TELL
ME
LIES

J.P. POMARE

Published in Australia and New Zealand in 2020
by Hachette Australia
(an imprint of Hachette Australia Pty Limited)
Level 17, 207 Kent Street, Sydney NSW 2000
www.hachette.com.au

10 9 8 7 6 5 4 3 2 1

 A catalogue record for this
book is available from the
National Library of Australia

ISBN: 978 1 8697 1816 9 (paperback)

Cover design by Christabella Designs
Cover photograph courtesy of Trevillion
Typeset in 12.2/16.5 pt Adobe Garamond Pro by Bookhouse, Sydney
Printed and bound in Great Britain by Clays Ltd, Elcograf S.p.A.

 The paper this book is printed on is certified against the
Forest Stewardship Council® Standards. McPherson's Printing
Group holds FSC® chain of custody certification SA-COC-005379.
FSC® promotes environmentally responsible, socially beneficial
and economically viable management of the world's forests.

Praise for *In the Clearing*

'*In the Clearing* is another breathtaking page-turner from the author of *Call Me Evie*. A dark, chilling, atmospheric thriller populated with mysterious and wonderfully flawed characters.'

Christian White, bestselling author of *The Nowhere Child*

'A chilling depiction of the ferocious hold exerted by a cult and its adherents. This is totally absorbing fiction, made all the more shocking by the realisation that these stories recur again and again in Australian society.'

Jock Serong, author of *The Rules of Backyard Cricket* and *Preservation*

'J.P. Pomare captivates in this haunting novel, *In the Clearing*. I was utterly gripped with the stories of Amy and Freya from start to finish, and fascinated by the unexpected way the two came together . . . A sure-fire bestseller.'

Sally Hepworth, bestselling author of *The Mother-In-Law* and *The Family Next Door*

'*In the Clearing* is SO good. I love "The Family"-esque vibe, the characters are so well drawn. It's such a great follow up to *Call Me Evie*!'

Ruth McIver, Richell Prize winner and author of the forthcoming *I Shot the Devil*

'I couldn't put it down. What a ride!'

Victoria Hannan, Victorian Premier's Unpublished Manuscript Award winner and author of *Kokomo*

Praise for *Call Me Evie*

'Almost nothing will turn out as it initially appears in this devastating novel of psychological suspense.'

Publishers Weekly (starred review)

'Read this one with the lights on, and keep Pomare on your radar.'

Kirkus Reviews

'I felt pure dread reading this book. Enjoyable, exquisite dread.'

Sarah Bailey, author of *The Dark Lake*

'It's a tight, compulsive, beautifully written thriller with echoes of Gillian Flynn, with characters that keep you guessing and a plot that keeps you turning the page.'

Christian White, author of *The Nowhere Child*

'a striking and suspenseful read'

Sydney Morning Herald

'the underlying threats, gripping storyline and unreliable narration in this debut novel will have you guessing and second-guessing until the very end'

Herald Sun

'a one-sitting kind of book, ideal for readers who enjoy fast-paced thrillers that keep them guessing'

Books+Publishing

'Pick this one up when you have plenty of time as you're unlikely to put it down after a few pages.'

Daily Telegraph

For Susan Dorne

PROLOGUE

'THE NEXT TRAIN to depart from Platform One is the 9:05 Flinders Street Line stopping all stations to Flinders Street.'

She takes the steps quickly, her hand slides along the rail. She is dishevelled, her mouth set in a pale line. There are a dozen or so people on the platform but she sets her sights on a man, standing there in a sweatshirt, a blue hat on his head and duffel bag slung over his shoulder. He has his back to her, gazing down at the phone in his hand.

Waiting in the shade on the platform, she glances back up the steps towards the street, then watches the man until the tracks begin to sing, a subtle high-pitched shriek that grows into a grumble.

The man looks up now, turning his head and watching down the tracks for the oncoming train. A light at first that grows brighter and brighter. It's loud now, so loud he doesn't hear her striding forward. The man turns back, raises his hands in defense, but half a second too late. She shoves him with all of her strength. The train is gliding into the station. His weight shifts; a gasp. Then he's falling. His body thuds against the concrete and rails. The train driver doesn't have time to apply the brakes; there is no time to do anything.

Reporter: Early reports have emerged of a yet-to-be-identified woman pushing a man in front of a train on a platform at Southbank station this morning. No further details have been released at this stage, but the attack appears to be random. We will have more for you later in the day. Police have warned there will be substantial delays for morning commuters on all trains passing through Southbank station.

PART ONE
THE
SOCIOPATH TEST

It is hard to believe that a man is telling the truth when you know
that you would lie if you were in his place.

H.L. Mencken

One Month Earlier

ONE

CORMAC IS DOING that thing again. *He* is the one asking the questions, not me. It's not entirely uncommon as a defence mechanism. If I'm asking the questions, I'm in control of the exchange and some people don't like that. Type A personalities need control as they fear being manipulated. When cornered, they might ask their own questions to pry control back. But it's not so simple with Cormac; he's not that kind of man. He's asking me questions because he's curious; he wants to get to know me before he can trust me. Despite the clinical setting, and the fact he's a client, trust is at the core of the relationship, trust is the silent contract we form. But I don't like the questions. I don't like giving up too much of myself.

'So you moved out here as a kid then?' he says in his breezy Irish lilt.

'Yes,' I say. 'When I was six, we moved to the city for my dad's work and I've been here ever since.'

'What did your dad do, then?'

'He was a professor.'

'They didn't need professors where you'd come from?' I keep his gaze. I show I'm still in control, even if he's asking me the questions.

3

'Well, they did, but he got a head of department role down here at a university.'

'Those bastards,' he says, with a grin. 'Nothing against your old man, but it was a head of department that booted me.'

It's healthy that he can laugh about it. Most young men would respond with more anger. 'Do you blame the head of department for what happened?'

'No, not him. I blame myself. I did it, no one else. I could have done something different to earn a little money.'

'The papers you wrote all earned As.'

'They did, you've done your homework.' Not homework: it was in the email from Adam Limbargo, the man who referred him on. I met Adam at university over twenty years ago, and he's still there lecturing in Anthropology. I've always felt like I've owed him a favour. He was a year or two older, but he always looked after me, when most older guys were more likely to try getting me into bed. There was a boozy night, I was stuck in the city and had lost my purse at a bar. Despite being in a drunken state himself, Adam put me in a taxi with enough cash for the fare.

Last time we met it was at a cafe over coffee. What I thought was an old friend hoping to catch up, I quickly realised, was a counselling session for him. You would be surprised how often it happens: I hear from someone out of the blue, wanting me to dispense free advice. He bought me a coffee, then told me about his problem. After that I didn't hear from him for months until he sent me this email.

Hello Margot,

It's been a while. I caught your guest lecture in April. I was at the back of the theatre and didn't have time to say hello but I did love your take on *Evil as a Necessary Ideal*. It is fascinating to think about the origin of the concept of evil, how it is really just a label for treatable behaviour that falls within the spectrum of Antisocial

Personality Disorder: sociopathy, psychopathy etc. But I'm not just writing to gush about your genius, Margot.

I'm sorry for the circumstances when we last caught up: I was in a dark place. Now I'm contacting you again because I have another favour to ask. I have a student who has been expelled from university. His name is Cormac Gibbons and to say he is remarkable is an understatement. Long story short, I believe Cormac could have an extraordinary career as a psychologist. The trouble is, he decided that it would be wise to write sixteen papers for other students in various courses – I should add they all earned A or A+ marks but that is beside the point. Most of the students have been punished in one way or another but the university had no choice but to move Cormac on. I don't understand people the way you do, Margot, but I know that Cormac was smart enough to comprehend the risks and consequences of his actions for a relatively small reward, and yet he still did it. He must have known he would get caught. This begs the question why would a student on a full scholarship risk his education for such a modest amount of money? It's risk-seeking behaviour at the least – it's almost as though he wanted us to throw him out. I'll leave it up to you, being the professional.

Cormac has agreed to see you and I'll be paying his fees if you can find time for the boy.

Can you help?

All the best,

Adam

I continue the session. 'And how did you get caught?'

'Someone came to me, I guess she knew what I was doing. She paid me for an essay and when I wrote it she took it to the head of department. *Entrapment*, you could call it.'

'So you blame her?'

'No,' he says.

His eyes move about the room. The vintage red cedar wardrobe I found in a store in Brisbane. The scrolled desk, tidy now but this morning it was cluttered with notes and bills. The small lockable filing cabinet where I keep recent notes from patients. And then his eyes settle on the painting on my wall. It's boring, but they're supposed to be boring. A landscape, rural Victoria, a dark barn in the distance. He turns back to me when I begin to speak again.

'Well, who do you blame then?'

'Why are you asking? Am I supposed to admit that I blame myself? You want me to accept responsibility. I told you, I do blame myself.'

'But do you really believe it or are you just telling me that?'

His eyes find the window now and fix there. 'Of course, I do.'

He smiles and it's clear he's used to the power of that smile, a Hollywood smile – strong jaw, generous lips, eyes a deep green – he knows what it can do, the doors it can open. But it doesn't work here.

I let my pen hover over the page of my pad. 'You blame yourself for what? The situation you and your sister are in or for losing your scholarship?'

'They'll take me back,' he says. 'That's why I'm here, that's why they organised our little meetings. That's why I'm looking into those pretty brown eyes.'

I keep a neutral expression, brush the compliment aside. 'We're talking about you today, Cormac, not me.'

'Of course. You get it all the time though, I'm sure.'

I push on. 'You were talking about your scholarship and the position you and your sister are in.'

'I was,' he continues. 'So I blame myself for the stuff with the university. But not for the position we are in. I know why we are here in Australia. I know why we're not back in Dublin, why I'm flat broke with no hope of making anything of myself.'

'And why is that?'

'My father.'

Like that, a breakthrough. A suspended breakthrough – this needs unpacking – but it's progress. I need to keep him talking.

'Tell me about him.'

'What do you want to know?'

'I want to know why you blame him for your current economic struggles.'

'*Economic struggles?*' he says, bemused. 'You ever worked in a kitchen?'

'No,' I say truthfully.

'Who do you think is the lowest of the low in a kitchen? One guess.'

'Who is it?'

'It's the *kitchen hand,* which is a fancy way of saying the guy that does the dishes.'

I eye the clock above the door. We have ten minutes left. 'Was that you, Cormac?'

'I scrubbed pots for seven hours. Chefs are all overworked, miserable pricks. They used to say stuff like "I need a clean pan stat" as if they were a doctor performing surgery and not just cooking someone else's steak. I could work forty hours scrubbing pans or write one essay and make more money.' This has to be an exaggeration; it didn't sound as if he was making *that* much money from the essays. I'm still sticking with the self-sabotage theory.

'So, let's take a step back. Why do you blame your father?'

'You know what my father did? You done your research?'

'No,' I say. 'I don't do research, Cormac, I let clients tell me. So I'm asking you, why *do* you blame him?'

'Now you're going Freudian on me, aren't ya?' Again that smile, his eyes half-closed. He cups his jaw, then slides his fore finger and thumb down over his stubble, pinching his chin. 'You're thinking I was competitive with him, somehow? I despise my father because I wanted to fuck my mum, right?'

I don't react, keeping a perfectly composed veneer. This is amateur stuff: an oedipal complex. He's mocking the practice now. It's juvenile but is he doing it to distract me? Or does he actually want to talk more about his parents' relationship. 'No, Cormac. That's an outdated idea. I'm sure your professors told you that. What we are doing now, what I am doing with you, is trying to understand who you are, your background, so we can make a plan moving forward.'

'A plan for what?'

'A plan for treatment. You said you wanted to go back to university. The only way they will take you back is if we can help you work through your issues.'

'Okay,' he says. 'You're right.'

'You want to be a psychologist, correct?'

'I like to learn about psychology. I don't know what I want to *be*.'

I scratch a note in my pad. *Interested in academic psychology.* 'Well, you will have to learn about yourself first.'

I glance up at the clock. Three minutes. I let the silence linger. Silence compels clients to fill it; stay silent enough and you tend to get honesty.

'So, tell me about your father.'

'You really want to know why I blame him ?'

'I do,' I say, turning a page of my pad.

He gives a small tired laugh. 'My father fell in love with the wrong woman.'

'What do you mean?'

'He fell in love with someone other than my mother and did something very bad.'

'What did he do, Cormac?'

He levels me with his gaze as if he's grown tired of the conversation. 'He took a knife and stabbed my auntie and my grandfather, and he tried to stab my mother, too. Mum survived but the others didn't.' My pen stops dead. My eyes flick up. He's looking at the window again, his nose is creased in a faint scowl. 'So you can write that down in your pad. Go on: *that* is why I blame my father. He is the reason we got as far away as we possibly could. He's the reason we're in Melbourne and not Dublin.'

Trauma, I think. Of course it is, of course that's why he doesn't feel he is good enough to be happy, to have a scholarship, or to maintain a healthy support network. *Trauma.* He probably blames himself in some way for the break-up of the marriage and his father's reaction. 'I'm sorry to hear that, Cormac.' He hides behind his humour, he tries to use flattery as a distraction, he doesn't trust men in positions of authority – it's beginning to make sense. He loved his mother, was raised by her, protected by her. 'And your mother?' I'm almost afraid to ask.

'She never really recovered. I don't know where she is now. She left us about a year ago. She would go out for days, and I'd come home and find her with a needle in her arm. She never adjusted after what happened to her sister and her dad.'

It's a bad time to stop but my next client will already be in the lobby. 'Okay, Cormac. We've come to the end of our time. I've got you again on Thursday. I want to continue this conversation then.'

'This coming Thursday?' he asks, rising. I stand too.

'Is that okay?'

'What time?'

'Ten o'clock.'

'Oh jeez, I've got some very important business to take care of at ten.' He smiles, to let me know he's joking. 'I'll be there.' He gently bumps my arm with his fist. The contact is too familiar, it's not professional, but I'm not going to admonish him after what he's just told me.

I look up into his green eyes. 'Don't be late,' I say. 'Oh, and Cormac, take ten minutes a day to write down anything you're thinking or feeling, especially when you feel any extreme emotion: anger, rage, ecstasy, elation. Just note it and write about it. Can you do that?'

'Alright, sure. Doctor's orders. Write my feelings down. Got it. See you Thursday at three.'

Before bringing in my next client, I go to Anna at reception, lean down and quietly ask, 'Has payment come through for Cormac?'

She clicks the screen. 'Yep, all paid up for the next few sessions.'

'Great. Give me two minutes, then you can send my next client through.'

I make a few more notes about Cormac's parents. I'm curious, so I quickly unlock my phone and search for the story. I find something. *Dublin double homicide, man in custody.* It's from years ago. But he's alive. Cormac's father is alive, or at least he was when he was arrested. He wasn't shot by the police and he didn't turn the knife on himself. *He fell in love with the wrong woman.* There is clearly a lot of trauma in his past, and in his family. Complex emotions he's suppressing and internalising, no doubt. Potentially self-blame too.

Now he is under an intense level of stress to raise his sister, to provide for her in a foreign place. He could justify the essay writing for others as a means to an end. I make one last note: *Father still alive in prison? Self-sabotaging or simply reckless?*

•

I get through my afternoon appointments, then set off for home. I park in our driveway, listening, waiting for the song to finish. *In Bloom* by Nirvana. I close my eyes for a few moments.

When I get inside, Gabe is hunched over a pan. I kiss him on the cheek. There's a bouquet of flowers on the table. *That's* a surprise.

'Flowers?' I say, taking them up, smelling them.

'Not from me,' he says, turning away from the pan, his lips twisted in an awkward smile. 'They've just come an hour ago.'

I take the card and turn it over in my hand. *Thanks for today, see you soon, Hudson x.*

'July,' I call into the cavernous house. 'July!'

'What?' her voice comes from upstairs, I look up and see her hanging over the banister, her hair falling around her face in dark curls.

'Come down here.'

She grunts. 'I'm busy.'

'Studying or talking to Hudson?'

'Studying.'

'Get down here now, July.'

It took her months to recover from her last break-up, her grades dropped, she was desolate. Now she's moved on, which I'm grateful for, but she seems to be even keener on this Hudson than the last boy.

'In the kitchen,' I say.

She comes through. 'What is it?'

'What did you do today?'

She looks guilty. I turn to Gabe, who shrugs.

'Were you at school?'

'Yes,' she says, dragging the word out, exaggerating. Then she notices the flowers on the kitchen bench.

'So if I call the school, they'll say you were there?'

'Oh my God, Mum, it's study leave. I don't have to be at the school all day.'

'So where were you?'

She looks to her father for help, as if Gabe is going to save her. Then she turns back to me. 'I was at the library in the city, okay? '

'Who were you with?'

Her cheeks are glowing now. 'I'm seventeen, Mum. I can hang out with whoever I like.'

'Were you with Hudson?'

She doesn't need to answer, I can see it in her face. 'Why didn't you tell us?'

'Because I didn't want you to make me go to school. No one else goes to school on study leave. We can study wherever.'

'That's beside the point,' Gabe contributes. 'We need to know where you are. You can't take off into the city on a whim. And how much study are you getting done with Hudson?'

'A lot, actually.'

'But he's finished school.'

'So?' she says. 'He's still studying.'

Studying law of all things. He went to school at Melbourne Grammar, Dad's a QC and now he's sending my daughter flowers. I laughed when July had told me, 'He's mature, Mum.' I asked what makes him mature. Her response: '*I don't know, he's focused on uni, and like he doesn't send selfies.*'

I grab the flowers, thrust them towards her. 'Here,' I say. 'Make sure you tell us next time.'

She smiles. I know that smile. It used to be the way she smiled for her father. She wouldn't dare smell them in front of us, but I can see she's tempted. 'Okay,' she says. 'Can I hang with him again tomorrow, then?'

I turn to Gabe, who simply shrugs. 'Hey, at least she's asking this time.'

We'll talk about this later, I think. 'Home by four,' I say, hating the fact I can't control my own daughter. 'Make sure you are actually studying, and keep your phone on.'

Prosecutor: 'Would the witness please read the document Exhibit A aloud?'

Simms: 'Ah sure, okay. Documentary evidence – Exhibit A: Personal diary extract

'She says I don't need to write about anything in particular, just to think about how I've been feeling lately and make a note of it. This week I was feeling a little down, but seeing Margot helped. It was probably the highlight actually, as sad as it sounds. She made me consider my history and how it affects me.

She tells me I'm clever, and tells me that when I'm better, when I am on top of things, I will be happy. When you think about my life and everything I've been through, it's impossible to believe my luck will change and everything will be fine. The past follows like a shadow, it stretches, growing longer and longer and darker and darker.

When she asks me if I blame anyone, I can't help but blame myself. It's always been my fault. If I answer honestly, if I really consider why I did what I did, the only answer is I am who I am. I'm made of all of my decisions and all the things that have happened to me. But now I have her. Now I have a reason to try harder.

The way she smiles at me, the way she tilts her head, her dark eyes fixed on me – I can't remember the last time someone made me feel so good about myself. But then she also challenges me too. I wonder if she knows that when she told me to write about my feelings I would end up writing about her.

What else is happening? Well, I feel like I can start working again soon, hopefully. I've not had to do work for

a while, and I wonder if I'll be able to sustain it. I applied for a few jobs and now I'm just waiting to hear back . . .'

Simms: 'And the rest is indecipherable.'
Prosecutor: 'Thank you.'

TWO

I'M HALFWAY AROUND 'the Tan', my local running track, when I pass a group of men. It's early and usually only the serious runners are out. Sometimes there are big runners' groups, huffing along in a cloud of breath. These men are chatting, little bursts of speech passing between them like static electricity. The sun is beginning to rise, it's too early for most but it's the best time of the day for me. I keep going, my pace is up. My watch tells me my heart rate is at one-twenty beats per minute, my cadence is at 160 and my kilometres per hour is sitting at eleven. There is the same man I've seen coming towards me a few times before.

'Morning,' he says, as I pass him.

'Good morning,' I say. Like me, he runs without headphones, without thumping music or podcasts, opting instead for the sounds of the city rolling out of bed, traffic starting up on Punt Road, the birds twittering in the trees.

I finish my lap then start up Domain Road towards home. After a short hot shower, I begin cooking breakfast for Gabe and the kids.

Gabe comes downstairs first. 'Morning,' he says. He reaches for the coffee, pours it into the blender and adds a tablespoon of butter.

'Still doing that thing?'

'It means you digest the caffeine slower.'

'I hate to break it to you, honey,' I say, touching his shoulder. 'Cavemen didn't drink coffee at all.'

He's unfazed. He sits down with the newspaper and sips the coffee while I turn his omelette. He eats it with asparagus and no toast – some trendy diet to try to get back to the belt notch he had in his twenties, but I can never get him out of bed for a run.

After Gabe's eaten, I prepare the kids' food and soon enough they emerge, one at a time. July gets up only after some fervent knocking.

'I'm awake,' she growls. *Where did that come from?* She never used to speak to me like this.

'You'll be late for school, July. Please come and eat your breakfast.'

'Okay okay, I'm getting up.'

July is seventeen but still eats *Coco Pops* for breakfast. Hard to believe she'll be a legal adult soon. Evan barely eats breakfast at all. He likes to take a muesli bar on the tram to school so he can get a few more minutes' sleep. He's usually up late, gaming with his friends online. He streams himself and has accumulated a sizeable following. We hear him some nights, he's so much more outgoing in the digital world than he is in real life, but he's a sweet kid.

•

I sublet half my office to a dietitian called Sarah. We share a receptionist and waiting area but have our own rooms. A hallway runs down one side of the building and Sarah's room is the first on the left, my much larger room the second. Sarah works closely with a cosmetic surgeon, which means her primary client base is made up of people pre- and post-surgery. From time to time, the surgeon refers them on to me as well. It turns out surgery alone isn't the answer to deep seated self-esteem issues. Who would have thought? Then there is Anna, our gorgeous young receptionist, who probably doesn't help with all the middle-aged insecurity.

South Yarra brings in a mixed bag of clients, but it's mostly garden-variety eating disorders, a few depressed housewives, blondes with menopause bobs more in love with their spoodles than their husbands, a few lonely self-absorbed bachelors, one woman who once a week needs to talk away her affair guilt. Then there are the borderlines: the narcissists, the addicts – usually gambling, cocaine, sex or social media, which bring a whole host of other conditions along with them.

Money can't buy you happiness, or style – despite the efforts of the Louis Vuitton faithful – but it can buy you a good listener and sound psychological advice. It can buy you a safe place to air your darkest secrets. Good psychologists are objective, not overly empathising but seeking to understand and help their clients. They are always prepared to learn, they're methodical and they save their notes to reflect on and help with similar cases in the future. For me the most important thing for the psychologist is a robust, process-driven, logical approach. It's less about feeling your client's pain, and more about understanding the mechanics of the human psyche. Your ego and your own life experience shouldn't be factors, although sometimes they are, and I'm always working to be the best I can be.

At the moment I'm researching more about Sociopathy or 'Antisocial Personality Disorder' for my next guest lecture – how to diagnose it, how to treat it, the history of our perception of the disorder. I'm reading a study before my first appointment of the day arrives: Xanthe.

She's there, sitting in the lobby at 10:15. Jeans torn at the knee, a long grey hoody. I know the things her clothes hide. Not the small kidney shaped birthmark on her neck, but those other pale lines on her skin, precisely placed inside the hem lines of her clothes.

'Xanthe,' I say. 'Come on through.'

She sits, eyes weary, arms wrapped around her waist. Defensive body language. One hand rises to her lips. Her thumbnail, what's left of it, is between her front teeth before she realises. She tears her hand away. She doesn't keep my gaze, instead turning to the window and looking at the street outside, blinking rapidly.

'How are you, Xanthe?' I begin.

'I'm okay. I'm doing okay,' she says.

'What's on your mind?'

'Right now?'

'Yeah.'

'I'm thinking about you, actually.'

'Me?'

'Yeah.'

'What about me?'

'You look pretty today,' she says, glancing up. I'm reminded of Gabe's old comics he keeps in our storage unit. *Harley Quinn*. I see something chaotic in Xanthe's smile, the way her cupid's bow lips curl up at the corners.

'We're talking about you today, Xanthe, not me. How have you been feeling lately?'

'Not good.'

'Not good?'

'No,' she says. 'I've been feeling anxious and worried.'

'Any more cutting?'

She pulls the sleeve of her hoodie up an inch revealing a razor thin scab.

'Is that new?'

'Two days ago.' It took a long time to get this level of trust. Only twice has she shown me any of her scars. Xanthe cuts, but it's manageable. The approach is to replace that impulse with another behaviour, slapping a rubber band against her wrist or folding paper. Xanthe also reports she has spectrophobia, a fear of mirrors. It's rare but people with extremely poor self-image can sometimes develop it.

'Was there anything happening when you felt like hurting yourself?'

'Jacob wasn't texting me, I was worried.' *Jacob*. The boyfriend. On again off again. Xanthe's moods oscillate wildly, and this relationship is the gauge of how far she swings. I'm working on building her self-worth, separating her sense of self from Jacob.

She continues speaking, staring at my hands where I hold my pen and pad. 'Mum has a place out in the country and it's empty all the time. I know where she leaves the key, so I thought about going there and just, I don't know . . . maybe, like, hanging myself.'

I swallow. Xanthe was prescribed antianxiety meds by her doctor when she was referred on to me. 'Have you been taking your medication?' I know the answer before I ask the question; I only need to look at the chewed nails, the wild searching eyes. She's as twitchy as a lizard.

'Umm, most days.'

Inwardly, I sigh. 'Most days?'

'It makes me drowsy.'

'I think you need to keep taking it, Xanthe. Just for now.'

Xanthe lies, that's another thing about her. She told me her brother died in a motorbike accident then she told me he died of leukemia. She told me a high school teacher molested her and then she acted as though she'd never said that at all. She's not had a good relationship with any men including her father, who left before she was born and she fought with her mum a lot and soon found herself booted out of home.

'I'll think about it,' she says, still staring at my hands. 'You always have nice pens,' she adds.

'It's always the same one,' I say. I've had it for years, and other clients have commented on it, too. It's the one my father gave to me when I graduated.

'It looks fancy.'

'We're talking about your medication, Xanthe.'

'Alright,' she says. 'I'll try to remember to take it every day.'

I glance down at the pen, and the inscription on the side. *Introspection is always retrospection.* Sartre's words, not Dad's, but now and then I read them and think about him. I think about the past.

THREE

JOE IS THERE in the waiting area after I see Xanthe out through the side exit. There is one entrance for patients arriving and a separate exit for patients leaving that runs into the alley beside the building and back out onto the street. Hunched over, filling the seat and plugging at the phone in his doughy hands is Joe. He looks up when I step into the waiting area. Joe grew up Catholic and his wife is still religious, even if he isn't. The only issue he has admitted to having is the fact he doesn't like how much time he spends on his phone – a complaint 90% of the population might make. Sometimes it frustrates his wife, he says. He will download a game and play it until 1 am while his wife sleeps next to him. Or sometimes he will go out and sit in the lounge and have a drink alone. His wife has woken in the night wondering where he is.

He lumbers in and is courteous enough to jam his phone into his pocket, but I can see his mind is still fixated on the game he was playing.

'So, what's new, Joe?'

'Not much, really,' he says.

'How is work?'

He frowns, looking down at his hands. 'It's okay.' *Okay,* but not *good.* 'I've had some trouble with sleep, lately.'

Games before bed? Or maybe booze? 'Are you finding you can't fall asleep or are you waking in the night?'

'Both, but it's mainly the dreams,' he says.

'What are you dreaming about?'

He licks his lips. 'Well, they're more like nightmares . . . I don't know.'

I swallow, giving him a few moments to gather his thoughts before continuing, but he doesn't. He's still frowning. Joe's job requires him to see a psychologist once a fortnight. He's a moderator for the photo-sharing social media platform Rad, which to me sounds exactly like hell. Whenever an image or video is flagged as inappropriate by users, someone like Joe must view the image and decide if it complies with Rad's terms and conditions. Joe routinely sees things like hate speech, violent attacks, and graphic pornography. Sometimes even child pornography, murder scenes, decapitations, torture scenes. Things deliberately posted to shock or scare users. One image might be innocuous and the next might be of a man being set alight. For years Joe has been viewing material that would likely cause a stress disorder in most people after just a few days. Each time a human views extreme violence, they become more desensitised to it. Think of abattoir workers, entirely comfortable torturing helpless animals. Think of the mass murderer who started out by slicing open the neighbourhood cats. Desensitisation kills empathy.

The interesting thing about Joe is that until he mentioned the nightmares he had seemed largely unfazed by his work.

'What's happening in the nightmares, Joe?'

'I'm angry, and I'm fighting someone.'

'Who are you fighting?' I ask.

'Well,' he says. 'That's the strange thing. I always wake before I find out. Or maybe I forget.'

'Are they hurting you?' I ask. 'Is that how the fighting starts?'

'Yeah, but then I win. I end up beating them.'

Interesting. I wonder if he's playing violent games at night? 'Is there anything you do before bed that might be bringing on these nightmares?'

'Not that I can think of. It's always the same. Someone grabs me and holds me down, their hands are around my neck, then I reach for a weapon and always seem to find something. A bat, or bottle.'

'Then what happens?'

'Then I hit them. Their grip loosens, I roll on top of them and I'm beating them. I just see dark hair and a broken shape beneath me.'

I find my eyes narrowing. I nod to let him know I'm listening, but he's looking at his hand.

'Last night I was using a fire extinguisher to beat them.'

Fire extinguisher, I jot down in my pad. 'Where are you?'

'Different places. Sometimes at home. Sometimes at work. Sometimes I'm even here in this room.'

The air cools a few degrees between us. His grey eyes look up from his hands, meeting mine now.

'Right. You're hurting someone in *this* room?'

'It changes every time, but yeah, I've been in this room in the dream.'

It becomes awkward for a moment, almost tense. I clear my throat. 'And is there any other pattern? Does it happen after a stressful day or an argument with your wife?'

'No,' he says, 'But I know the images are doing something to me. People are always telling me they will. I thought I was perfect for the job. I saw lots of things growing up and I'm not soft or anything but . . . maybe it is getting to me.'

Dark hair, broken and bloody on the floor of this room. *I* have dark hair. Joe is looking down at his hands again. When I first met him, I had to research the conditions associated with this role. Most people can't work in social media content moderation for more than a couple of years, and many will experience post-traumatic stress and a host of other debilitating mental conditions. *That's* what was so fascinating about him: he has never shown signs of PTSD and has few anxiety issues. He's got a mild drinking problem, smartphone addiction and other common twenty-first century ailments, but he's generally well adjusted. He even felt genuine guilt when he found someone's phone on a train and took it home, thinking he might keep it. Eventually the owner realised they'd lost it, called the number and arranged to pick it up. But now, he's dreaming horrible scenes, which means he's probably been disassociating, hiding his interior world from his daytime life.

It is completely unfair that people are forced into this sort of work to make a living, a pittance, really, compared to the emotional turmoil they suffer. Joe is one of the lucky ones who gets some support; in other parts of the world workers have none.

I have to ask the question. 'Joe, have you ever had an urge to hurt anyone?'

'No,' he says. 'Not for years.'

'So you have in the past?'

'Just road rage, angry at other fans at the footy, that sort of thing. I never really hurt anyone back then.'

Back then.

'Do you think you need time off, maybe? A week or so away to *reset.*'

'Nah,' he says. 'I'll be fine. If I ever have trouble sleeping, I've found taking a drive helps. If I go for a decent drive, fill the car up or just roll through the city, it makes me sleepy and when I get home and have a whisky I nod off straight away.'

'Do you think that's safe, driving when you're already tired?'

'Roads are quiet, it beats just lying in bed at home.' He coughs then, loud and sudden as a rifle shot. He covers his mouth with a fist, then thumps his chest.

I pause a moment, sipping my water. Then I hold out the tissues to him but he waves them away.

'I'm fine,' he says, still breathless.

I glance down at my notes. 'If you're on your phone before bed, it can speed your mind up, make it hard to sleep. Do you think maybe you could try reading for half an hour instead?'

'I never liked to read,' he says. Again, he has that pained expression, almost like he's grinning through kidney stones, his lips pulled back and big yellow teeth exposed. 'I've never been able to concentrate that long, you know. But I guess there's no harm in trying.'

'I think that would be healthy. Try to find a book you love; it can be a real boon for your sleep. And Joe, do you ever have negative thoughts during the day at your work?'

'You ask me this every time and the answer is the same. *Everyone* has negative thoughts.'

'And I'll tell you again, Joe, the negative thoughts I'm talking about are thoughts of harming yourself or anyone else.' If he doesn't have any negative thoughts, it's clear he's disassociating at work.

'I have negative thoughts every day. I have nothing but negative thoughts. That doesn't mean I'm not happy. I am. And I would never harm myself.'

It's eerie, vaguely ominous. I push on. 'And other people.'

'I can't say I would never harm anyone else. It would be a lie.'

I study his face. He wears a dumb, unreadable expression. I let the silence settle but he is immune to awkwardness. 'Can you elaborate on that?'

'Well if someone was going to hurt my family, of course I would harm them, but it wouldn't be because of negative thoughts.'

'What are the negative thoughts about specifically, Joe? Anyone in particular.'

A flicker of irritation. 'Well, I think about how some people exploit children or hurt each other, the usual stuff.' I can't explain why, let's call it professional intuition, but I feel like Joe is lying to me.

•

At the end of the day, I walk down to where my car is parked and I see Adam Limbargo. He's striding from one of the university office buildings toward a taxi.

'Adam,' I call, rushing to catch him. 'Adam, hi.'

'Oh,' he says, with one hand on the door handle. 'Margot, hi.'

'I just wanted to say, I can't give you specifics, but I have agreed to counsel Cormac.'

His brow creases. 'I'm glad to hear, but look I've got to run.' Then he's dropping into the backseat of the taxi, and it's pulling away from the curb.

I drive home. I notice that a car has been following me from where I was parked near my office. I block it out, knowing this is a common psychological experience; a white Toyota in the rear-view mirror, then ten minutes later you look up and see a similar car and are convinced someone is following you. But now that I'm focusing on it, I realise they've turned down our quiet street. I indicate, pull into our driveway and it rolls past. I sit there for a moment watching the rear-view mirror for the driver, but I see only a dark silhouette. Curious, I sit there thinking for a moment before heading towards the house.

FOUR

YOU GET THE bad boys out of the way in your teen years, then find someone kind and caring to marry. My relationship prior to Gabe was tumultuous, something of a bad boy to say the least, but most other love interests were like Gabe: calm and easy, *safe*.

He was the one that asked my father before he proposed – a terrifying prospect if you knew my father back then, an *academic* psychologist with an interrogating gaze and sarcasm that could draw blood. Gabe called him rather than asking in person because by that stage my father was living in Vancouver, undertaking a residency at a university there. Growing up with him, I always felt a little like one of his test subjects. Something to be studied and understood, rather than cared for and emotionally nourished. He was always asking me questions, studying my responses. He was also incapable of uttering the words, *I don't know*. If he was ever confronted with a problem he didn't have the answer to, he was much more likely to say something like, 'Well I suppose the answer would be . . .' or 'One would assume that . . .' A far cry from my Gabe, who was so uncertain, so careful and kind. Gabe was someone who didn't kiss me until our third date and wouldn't have fucked me if I hadn't dragged him onto me after a long night of cocktails in the city.

Gabe hasn't changed at all in that time, he's just as rocksteady, just as moderate and conservative.

July is at the kitchen bench, when I get inside. 'So, when is he coming for dinner?' Gabe asks, teasing July about Hudson. I don't want to pressure July or rush her any more with this kid. If he meets us and they *do* eventually break up it will be even harder for her.

'Soon,' she says, her expression somewhere between excitement and frustration.

'Have *you* met *his* parents?'

'Dad,' she says. 'Stop, please.'

We eat dinner together, a peaceful family meal. I watch Gabe for a moment and everything seems perfect, balanced. Everything is in its right place. And for the first time in what seems like months, when we turn back the covers and climb into bed, I pull Gabe's face to mine, press our lips together and find him responding in kind. He's almost surprised. He peels my underwear away, reaching for me like we're in our twenties again.

Afterwards we just lie there in silence and eventually Gabe says, 'Can you smell that? It smells like some sort of chemical.'

And that's when we hear the explosion downstairs.

FIVE

GLASS DETONATES. GABE sits up suddenly.

'What the hell was that?'

'It sounded like a window,' I hiss.

'Too loud to be a window,' Gabe says.

I fling the covers off. My heart slams against my ribs like a fist. The room is dark.

'Should I call the police?' I say, reaching for my phone.

He rolls over, his feet finding the floor. I can hear crackling, now. The room fills with light and I see him, his arm still touching the lamp.

'I can smell it now,' I say, my voice quick and urgent, the feint pungent odour growing stronger.

'Smoke,' Gabe says, uncertain. Then the house screams. The smoke alarms all going at once. I hear a door open in the hall.

'Fire!' he shouts. 'Quick, let's get out.'

I roll from bed, pull on track pants and a t-shirt then take off down the hall. 'Get July. I'll get Evan,' he says quickly, but by the time I get to her room, July is already charging through the door, fully dressed.

'What's going on?' she says, clutching my arms.

'Fire downstairs!'

We sprint in a chain down to the bottom level as black smoke fills the house. My heart pounds and my lungs itch. I lift my top to my mouth and breath through the fabric. Gabe and Evan are behind us, all running towards the door. My phone is hard against my ear.

'What's your emergency?' a voice says.

'Fire,' I say, turning, catching a glimpse of the flames climbing the wall in the lounge. I'm first to the front door and find it's already open, framing the darkness of night outside. 'At our house.' I give the address, leaping down the steps to the lawn. Me, July, Evan and . . . and . . . where's Gabe? He hasn't come out.

'A fire crew will be with you soon,' the woman says.

Gabe, I realise, is still inside. I rush back to the front door and into the house. The smoke is so thick I can barely see. I find the shape of him, a dark form moving through the murk. 'Gabe!' I scream. 'Get outside now.'

I get close, coughing. My eyes water but I can make out the steel pot in his hands. He's hopelessly trying to douse the flames. A rage comes over me, swift as thunderclap. I catch his arm as he turns to head back to the sink. He's coughing too. 'Gabe! Get out right now!'

'Our home . . .' he says, followed by another fit of coughing.

'*It's insured*,' I scream. 'Don't be an idiot, get out.' I don't need to tell him it doesn't matter about the house if we're dead. I try to drag him, but he resists, pushing me off.

'You stubborn shit, get out now!' He gives in, grabbing my arm, and running with me for the door. We both emerge, tears streaming. My eyeballs sting and my throat feels full of steel wool. I cough, hunching over my knees. Now Gabe rushes for the garden hose. In the dark of the night, with only the fire and the streetlights, I stand with one hand clamped to my forehead and the other on my hip watching my husband rushing back towards the window of my study. His shadow stretches back over the lawn as a fire rages in my home.

He aims the hose inside, spraying the flames. The fire is so loud, so bright that at first I don't register the sirens, the red and blue lights strobing the empty street. Then I notice something. We'd run straight over it when we left. A sheet of paper on our front step. I move towards the door. It was open. *Why was it wide open?* Gabe had locked it before we went to bed.

'Mum!' July calls. 'What are you doing?'

I turn back. She's near the front gate, the spaghetti straps of her top are dark like the lines dividing a doll's limbs. Evan is beside her and they're both watching me. I continue on, the heat overwhelming. I crouch and snatch the sheet of paper, then rush back towards them. Across the road, a light has come on inside a house. Soon enough, neighbours will be emerging. Our fire alarms continue to howl. I look down at the sheet of paper and a cold finger runs over the back of my neck.

'What?' July asks, but before she can see, I press the sheet to my chest, hiding the image. 'What is it?'

I'm trying to think what to tell her when I fold. I can feel something rush up my throat. I spray the Alfredo and pinot noir from dinner over our lawn. My throat burns and it's hard to breathe. The piece of paper shows a man. Or the body of a man – but where his head should be, there's – it's gone. There's blood, bone, the inside of a skull all splattered on the wall behind him. It has to be fake, but it seems so real.

I straighten up, the image still clutched in my fist. Firefighters are rushing about us, but suddenly I have the urge to protect my family: the image might be fake, but the fact remains, someone wanted to hurt us. I find myself pulling my children against me, kissing the crowns of their heads, watching as Gabe is pushed back, led away by one of the firefighters. Their hoses blast into the blaze and soon it's only smoke. Smoke, glass, and our house, one corner blackened by flame. Morning is still hours away, as the police arrive. There will be no sleep tonight.

SIX

'SO, YOU HEARD a crash – then what?'

We're all on the curb, one officer is talking to me, another is talking to Gabe. The children are nearby but they've separated us to gather statements. The window to my home office was smashed and fire fighters, I'm certain, will confirm the blaze started there. Someone threw something through the window and it set the house on fire. But the first place the police will look is at us, the occupants. I wince, thinking about my locked bureau, the irreplaceable notes from patients that I've accumulated through the years. Most I kept here, some at my office and some in storage.

I talk the cop through our night: we didn't have any candles lit, we didn't leave any heaters on. No fighting or *domestic* issues. I hand her the photo I found. She looks at it for a moment, holding it in her latex-gloved hand. Then she looks back to me.

'It was on your doorstep?'

'I saw it when we were outside, I wish I hadn't picked it up—' I shake my head.

'Have you seen this image before?'

'No,' I say. 'Never.'

'Is there anyone you know that for any reason might want to do this? Any threats, any enemies?'

I can think of a lot of people who would do this in general. Through the years I've dealt with verified psychopaths, sociopaths, borderlines and narcissists. But none who would have my address, and none who, as far as I'm aware, would want to hurt me specifically.

'No,' I say. 'No one springs to mind.'

I glance at Gabe. I can see his lips moving, his eyes downcast. Insurance will cover the damage, but how long will it take? Will anything be salvageable inside? How far did the fire spread from my study? And what about all the electrical hazards, the fumes from the fire, the structural integrity? Amongst the barrage of thoughts and concerns, I think about my work. All the clients tomorrow; how will I face the day when the sun rises?

Sitting on the curb, July's arm hangs across Evan's shoulders, whose head is down, his knees pulled to his chest, crying into his forearm. He's got the structure of a man now, tall with gangly limbs, but he hasn't filled out yet. He still has a youthful face with spots of acne near the dark curls of his hairline. I can't help but be buoyed by the way they're supporting each other. All of July's study notes are inside, and Evan's gaming set-up. They've both lost a lot.

The officer places the sheet of paper with the image in a ziplock bag and writes on the label with a sharpie.

'There was one other thing,' I add, before I sign the statement she has written out for me. 'I felt like someone followed me home from work today. A white Toyota, but, I don't know . . . maybe I was imagining things.'

'Any plates?'

'No, like I said, I didn't think much of it.'

'Model?'

'It looked like a Camry I guess, it was a sedan. Newish.'

'See the driver?'

'No,' I say. 'No, sorry, it's probably a coincidence.' I can see her chew the inside of her cheeks, a slight pout.

'It is likely a coincidence, yes,' she says. 'But if this is arson, I'm going to need you to try remembering more details, other things you might have noticed.'

Before we leave, another cop arrives at the scene. A rugby build, balding with an island of clipped blond hair running down the middle of his head. He introduces himself.

'Detective Simms,' he says. A big man with a surprisingly small voice, the voice of a wind instrument. 'Don't worry we will get to the bottom of this.'

•

The hotel is nice. Closer to the office than our home. Close enough that I could probably walk. I have some work clothes I keep at the office, and thankfully had a change of clothes in my car, but not enough to last more than a few days. We get a two-bedroom suite on level twelve of the Ramada Inn. The kids are sharing a double. Considering they're both teenagers, it's a little awkward, but this is the only room so close we could find on such short notice.

Gabe is onto the insurance company, I can hear his bare feet striding a worried track in the old hallway carpet outside the door. His murmurings are soft, so as not to wake other guests but still firm and anxious. He's trying to find out what our policy covers before we go spending too much money on accommodation, new clothes, provisions.

He falls silent in the hall and his footsteps come closer. The door opens and he silently walks inside.

'So, they're *very sorry* to hear about the fire. They'll be waiting for the report from the fire department before they can pay out on any claims, but accommodation, clothing, etc. are all covered if it is accidental or criminal arson. She made it clear that if it was arson caused by an occupant it wouldn't be covered.'

'Kids were in bed. I don't think that will be an issue.'

'You know how slippery they are. Remember how long it took when the Audi was stolen?'

'I remember,' I say, pulling him against me. He doesn't squeeze me back, I can feel the fatigue in his bones.

'Let's try to get some rest,' he says.

'Who do you think would do it? Who would put that picture there?'

'I don't know. I really don't think they were trying to hurt us,' he says. 'Why else would they leave a picture, why would they try to scare us like that, if they thought we would all die? And they left the door open, right?'

'That's the most concerning part,' I say. 'It's like it was a plan. I don't know why anyone would do this, but with a little luck, hopefully they left fingerprints or DNA or something.'

'Then they can lock the bastard up and drop the key in a volcano,' he says, with a tired huff of laughter.

If only it were that simple.

I set my alarm for nine. I won't run in the morning, but I'll still go to the office. We tuck ourselves into the crisp sheets. Soon I hear the slow rhythmic breathing of Gabe sleeping. I plug my headphones in and listen to a podcast, hoping to distract my mind enough to fall asleep.

•

Gabe wakes me. I slept through my alarm, or rather I woke, stabbed blindly at my phone to silence it and fell straight back to sleep. It's ten to ten, which means Cormac will be walking into the practice in ten minutes.

'Shit,' I say. 'I've got to run. I'll Uber so you can use my car.' I pull on my track pants and t-shirt. I'm ordering an Uber when Gabe speaks.

'Take the day off, Margot. You need to rest; we've got to sort out the insurance.'

I pause, thinking about Cormac. He is such an intriguing case and we're making progress. 'No, I've got to go. You're not going to work?'

'No,' he says. 'I've already called for the day off. The kids are staying here, too.'

'Where are they?'

'July is on the phone to Hudson in bed.'

She posted a video of the fire to Instagram, and Mum saw it so that's how she found out. I've had others calling and messaging. Evan is down at breakfast.'

I glance down at my phone. I've got messages from friends. Linda, my wine buddy, has messaged offering up her apartment in the city for us to use.

'I thought we got the message through to the kids about being mindful of what they're putting online. She shouldn't be posting stuff like that. It'll only make people worry and we still don't know who did this to us.' I don't know exactly where this frustration comes from, but I suppose it has something to do with the fact anyone could be watching, even the person who set it.

'It could have been electrical,' he says. 'There's no way to know yet.'

'And what about the image on the doorstep?'

My phone vibrates. The Uber is downstairs. I quickly brush my teeth, tie my hair back, then go. I do my make-up in the car and call Anna, the receptionist.

'Hi, it's Margot.'

'Good morning, Margot,' her voice bright.

'Look, can you put my 10 am in my office? I'm going to be five minutes late. Also, I have a change of clothes hanging up in the wardrobe. Could you grab it out and keep it at the front desk.'

'Sure.'

'Won't be long.'

The driver senses my urgency, speeding through the streets. It's three minutes past when we pull up. It's five minutes past when I emerge from the bathroom in the spare clothes. I look in the mirror, flushed, self-conscious, and stride into my room.

Reporter: A house in the inner east has been the target of a suspected arson attack in the early hours last night. After finding evidence of a Molotov cocktail, police have ruled out all other potential causes of the blaze that has left a family without their home. The fire began between 12 and 1 am and police are asking any potential witnesses to come forward.

SEVEN

'CORMAC, I'M *SO* sorry,' I say. I know it's unprofessional and if it was anyone else I would have rescheduled the appointment, but after the last session I knew I couldn't miss it. He's standing with his back to the door, reading a book from my shelf. He turns back. I recognise the book straight away *Men, Women and the Brain*. It's my book.

'Oh don't worry, Mrs. I've been reading.'

'You can stay ten minutes longer at the end of our session. I don't have anyone until eleven-twenty.'

'That's kind of you,' he says. Holding the book up he adds, 'you wrote this?'

'I did.'

He pokes out his bottom lip and gives a small nod of approval before sliding the book back onto the shelf. He comes over to his seat. 'It wasn't on our reading list at university.'

'No,' I say. I take up my pad and sit down across from him. Some psychologists don't like a pad as it can be seen as a barrier, and it can influence the client's response. They make their notes between sessions. That's not me. Writing notes helps to order my thoughts while we talk. I have rows and rows of notepads, filed away. Some were lost in the fire, but many more are here in the filing cabinet in my office or in our storage facility, collected over the years, so I can always refer back to past cases.

'Long morning, was it?' he says with a smile.

'Something like that,' I say, failing to keep the note of anxiety out of my voice.

I see his features shift, concern in his eyes. 'What is it?'

'Nothing, it's fine. It was a long night.'

'Right,' he says. 'Well, have you written any other books?'

'Not yet, but I've got another guest lecture later in the year and I'm interested in the subject, so I might write about that.'

'What is it?'

'I'm researching Antisocial Personality Disorder.'

'Sociopaths?' he says. 'Interesting.'

'So how are you?' I say, changing the subject.

'I'm alright. I got another job.'

'You did? That's good to hear.'

He licks his lips and tilts his head. 'It's a crap job, but I need the money. At least I'm not working in a kitchen. I got it the day I applied.'

'That's good. Where is it?'

'It's a cafe. I applied for the kitchen hand, but the owner must have liked me 'cause she said she'd have me waiting tables instead.'

'Good place to work?'

'It is; good people. The barista is on my case already and it's only been one shift.'

'They don't like you?'

'No, the opposite as a matter of fact,' he says, again flashing a smile. I feel a pang of something in my chest.

'A romantic interest?'

'Possibly. I think she's quite eager, actually. Is that arrogant to say?'

'Not if it's the truth. Oh well, this job will keep you busy until your talents are needed elsewhere.'

'Talents,' he says, exhaling. 'What talents?'

'You're very intelligent, Cormac. Adam Limbargo seems to think you're exceptionally talented.'

He smiles. 'I've been hearing that my whole life, but it doesn't pay the bills or put food on the table. Whenever I hear "you're talented" I always think it simply means I can achieve the same as everyone else but with marginally less effort.'

'That's one way of looking at it.'

'You see it different?'

'I see someone who can do more than most people, someone that can solve problems, someone that can change lives.'

He laughs at me, but there's no meanness in it. 'You see more in me than I see in myself, that's for sure.'

I realise I've forgotten about the fire, I realise that for the last five minutes I've felt normal, like someone didn't almost kill me and my family last night. I knew it was a good idea coming in today.

'In our last session we were talking about your father.'

'My dear ole pappy. Yes.' He runs his fingers back through his straight brown hair.

'What was it like growing up with him?'

He thinks for a moment. 'Dad was a good man,' he begins, lacing his fingers together and rubbing his hands back and forth. 'I know that sounds strange – about a murderer, but I mean that's what people called him before he did it, *a good man*. He was a little eccentric, but he did right by everyone. He had all the things that made you a "good man" in Ireland in the nineties.' He makes air quotes with his index and forefingers. 'He grew up without a dad. That's where I think his own problems stemmed from. He grew up with a mum who didn't love him. He was working class but smart. Street smart, you'd say.'

'Did your mum tell you this?'

'Yeah, and I remember. I always felt closer to him than Mum for some reason.'

I was the same, I think.

'So he was working in the mines most of his life. Raising us kids. He liked to have a drink, and he would come home late. One night when he is still at the pub, my mam suddenly comes into our room. She said we're leaving. She said that Dad has a new woman and he can't have us kids, so she drives us up north. I still remember it, clearly.'

I'm engrossed, his story has taken me away from my own problems. Childhood trauma shapes so much of our adult biases; it forms the people we become. Cormac is reckless but brilliant. He's resentful of wealth and the powers that be. I'm seeing a pattern emerging. I can see why Adam Limbargo took a shine to him. Adam himself grew up working class. His mum, an English teacher, gave him a good brain, and his dad, a racehorse trainer, gifted him a mild gambling addiction, a problem that grew the older he got. That was the last thing Adam and I caught up about: he wanted help for it.

'So she takes you away not to protect you, but to keep you from your father?'

'That's right. That's the way I see it. She didn't force his hand or anything, but she poked the bear.'

'Poked the bear?'

'I don't want you to think I'm apologising for my father in anyway. There's no excuse for what he did. But my mum knew he was a little unstable. She wasn't protecting us, I don't believe that. I don't believe Dad would hurt me. She was using us to get back at him.'

'And the other woman?'

'I hated her. Maybe I still hate her. Maybe she didn't realise he had a family, but still—' white-lipped, teeth gritted, frustration is welling inside of him '—if it wasn't for her we might have been different. I might still have a family. But Mum barely even gave the other woman a second thought. She blamed Dad.'

'Then what happened?'

He closes his eyes and opens them, a beat longer than a blink. 'Then we get to my grandparents' house. Mam's sister still lived there. I remember getting inside and thinking it's so warm. The fire was blazing. Grandpa was out in the yard, chopping wood. I had my bear under my arm and my younger sister was so little she was barely walking by that stage. I remember Mam and Grandpa arguing. I remember them putting us upstairs in a room with toys then I could hear them arguing louder.'

'You remember it all clearly?'

He licks his lips. His eyes rise to the ceiling.

'I can see it all. I can hear it. I can feel the hard edges of the toy tractor I was pushing about the room. Then I can hear a car on the street. Mam saw, and knew it was Dad. She burst into the room, grabbed us hard by the wrists and dragged us to her own car parked up the alleyway around the back of their flat, then went back. We could hear shouting coming from inside. It was late, dark out. We were in the car. I'd told Mum we wouldn't get out, no matter what. The door slammed open at the back of the flat. Mam was there screaming.' He pauses, recalling that time. 'She was just screaming and screaming and—' he frowns deep now, his eyes almost closed '—I don't know what happened in between. I don't even think I saw Dad. I only saw Mum with blood all over her and she kept saying his name – she was screaming. Then we were speeding away from the house. And Dad was outside and there was even more blood on him and he was just watching the car and I was watching him out the back window, which, if you want a metaphor, you're unlikely to find a more apt one. Dad red-handed, Mum stealing us away from him. I was still young and now I know that you don't form real memories until you're seven or eight so I don't know how much of it is my memory and how much is images stored from the nightmares I have about it.'

I wince internally, beginning to realise how complex Cormac's issues are. We inherit all sorts of traits from our parents. I always wanted to please my own father; that's why I ended up as a psychologist – to impress him, I suppose. Psychologists always have trouble understanding themselves – psychologists *see* other psychologists for this very reason. I've had patients who were practicing psychologists who failed to see how events in their childhood shaped them as adults. It's a professional blind spot.

'Do you think your mother changed then? Was she different afterwards?'

I'm losing him now. I can see the vagueness in his eyes. Very intelligent people often intellectualise their emotions. They speak about them like they're happening to someone else. They displace their feelings with thought and logic. He smiles. 'I think when you see something like that, it will change anyone.'

'And your father, where is he now?'

'When he was done killing my grandparents, he ah—' a pause, his eyes seem to shine for a moment. 'Well he turned the knife on himself.'

But he survived, otherwise the article would have made it clear he was dead, and not *in custody*.

'But he's alive?'

'If you can call it living.'

'So he went to prison, then?'

'Yep. Last I heard, he was still there,' he says. 'But I'll never see him again.'

I glance at the clock. It's been forty minutes, but I could talk about this all day. 'I'm so sorry,' I say. I find myself leaning over the table, reaching out. My hand is on his before I can stop it and I'm squeezing his hand in my own. He looks at our hands touching, then up into my eyes. I gently pull away. Contact can be helpful if applied in a professional and courteous way, initiated often by the client but not always. I know I can come across as cold and clinical, so a brief touch can help.

'It's fine. I'm fine,' he continues in his thick Irish accent. 'It was years ago, and I'm a man myself now. It's funny though, sometimes I feel like I see him, you know? He was a big balding man. Just a few days ago, I was walking home from here, actually. I was heading down to the train station and I felt like someone was following me. He was quite far back but every time I turned, I thought to myself he looks a little like him. I was imagining it of course, but still.'

My attention jags. *A tall bald man.* 'So you thought someone was following you?'

'Umm, well, probably not. I just noticed him. He walked the same way as me all the way to the train station then got on.'

'He got on your train?'

He frowns now. 'What's this got to do with my dad? Or with helping me get back into school.'

'Well, we're diving deep, Cormac. I know you think your problems stem from tangible, easily understood realities of surviving in the world. For example, your need for money. But there are plenty of ways to make money. We're trying to figure out why you chose a particularly reckless way of doing it. You might have some other things troubling you, other reasons linked to your formative years.'

'And what makes you think I can get better?'

'I think we're working through it. We're trying to figure it out together. The fact you took a job in a cafe tells me there is progress. It tells me you are prepared to take a conventional, low-risk approach.'

'I'm getting boring, aren't I?'

'I don't think so: you're gaining control.'

'Gaining control? I'll remember that when my sister is hungry, or my landlord ups the rent.'

'No, having control doesn't directly pay the bills, but it means you are more likely to keep a job. Do you think your sister might find work, too?'

'I don't think so,' he says. 'I'm looking after her but she supports me as well. She'd do anything for me, but I don't want her working. She needs to focus on school. She's the last thing keeping me here, you know. If I ever lost her, I'd grab a taxi and take the next flight out. I wouldn't hesitate.'

I make a note. *Family only attachment to place, flight risk.*

'So why were you really late?' he asks. My heart sinks again, and I see that image, the missing head, I see the flames and I'm reminded of a hard fact: someone wanted to hurt us.

'We had a fire at our house last night. No big deal.'

'A fire? What sort of fire?'

The breathless roar, flames climbing the walls. I think of the bottle someone threw – *a Molotov cocktail,* Gabe had said. 'It was big. We're staying in a hotel now until the insurance people have been through. It's all a headache.'

'Oh shit, I'm sorry Mrs. This was last night?'

I nod.

'I feel lousy now. You didn't have to come in to see me – I ain't even paying. You could have charged the dean for the appointment and I wouldn't tell.'

Adam probably owes me an appointment fee anyway, I joke to myself. 'I have ethics protocols which I must adhere to.'

'And what a shame that is,' he says, with a laugh. I feel that familiar flush in my cheeks. *Keep it professional, Margot.* For the second time he's made a comment that could be construed as inappropriate. I stare straight into his eyes. 'Sorry, I shouldn't talk like that. What I'm saying is, that's a big deal; you shouldn't be in here dealing with reprobates like me.'

'Well you're certainly *not* a reprobate and it's a good way to take my mind of things.'

'I don't have much in the way of money but why don't we get a pint? I feel like you could do with the afternoon off.'

I swallow. I've let it get too casual in this session. 'No, Cormac. That's kind of you, but it wouldn't be a good idea for me as your psychologist to socialise.'

'Right you are,' he says. 'I thought it was a long shot. Another time then.'

I purse my lips and give a small nod. 'Maybe one day,' I say, knowing it's very unlikely. 'For now, I want you to tell me more about your mother, and how your relationship changed after the incident with your father.'

Prosecutor: 'Would the witness now please read the document Exhibit B aloud for the court?'

Simms: 'Documentary evidence – Exhibit B: Personal diary extract.

'Why why why do I have to open my mouth and say things like that? I clearly made her uncomfortable. I didn't mean anything by it, really, but I couldn't help myself. I've been feeling lonelier than usual and I was too open. It's impossible not to wonder what she's thinking, what is going through her head when she sees me, her eyes on my face, asking me questions. It's an easy way to fall in love.

I went to the shop today, and when I took a jar of pickles from the shelf it slipped from my fingers and exploded, juice running out beneath the shelves, down the aisle. Someone came rushing over. It was a man with white hair and large confused eyes. He left and came back with a mop and I just stood there. I insisted on paying, I felt so bad, but the impulse to destroy, seeing the broken glass, the jagged edges, there was something satisfying about it.

It feels a bit like that with Margot. Every time I open up a little more, every time I divulge more history, more feelings, more secrets, I grow closer to her. It feels like I'm risking something but what's life without risk? She is opening up a little too. We made skin contact, a small, tiny act but it was something. At first, she barely responded to my questions and it was perfunctory but as we've gotten to know each other more, we've become like friends, and that's why I thought I could treat her like a friend. But when I said those stupid words, that easy smile fled her face and the professional veneer was back up. Am I just a project for her? I know she treats me different to others, I'm sure of it, but maybe it's not a friendly relationship, maybe I'm like her science experiment or simply a problem to solve—'

Prosecutor: 'You can stop there.'
Simms: 'Right.'

EIGHT

ON SATURDAY MORNING we move into an Airbnb close to home. A four-bedroom place, with a modern fit-out and large rooms with vaulted ceilings. Gabe rolled his eyes at the Ikea prints on the walls of the bedroom, but other than that it is perfectly adequate for our purposes. It's fifteen hundred dollars a week, money from our credit card, so I only hope the insurance covers it all. That afternoon Gabe and I drive five minutes from the Airbnb to our home to find that they've secured it – apparently people loot burnt-out homes. It's wrapped up in police tape and boards have been nailed over the smashed windows. A locksmith has been and changed the locks.

We're not allowed inside, not even to collect basics – Evan's computer, July's makeup and study notes. Even if it was safe to enter, which clearly it's not, it's still a crime scene. But it will do Evan good to have a break from gaming. It's not as though he can't live without it: we enforced a weeklong ban last year and managed to get him down watching TV with us. He even read a book. And he didn't lose any subscribers on his Twitch gaming channel. So no harm, no foul. It's been a couple of days now, though, and he's already nagging us to buy a new set-up. The water damage from the hoses has likely ruined his computer, anyway.

'It's all boarded up now, folks,' Simms says, as we stand out on the lawn, eyes roaming the damage. 'I can send you the report, but the property damage is extensive. There's a lot of structural work required. Might be a knock down, rebuild situation.'

Gabe lets out a huff of frustration. 'So we're talking potentially years?'

'I'd guess, maybe a year or so. But I'm not here to talk to you about the damage – we're trying to find out who might have caused it. On this front we've got one or two updates.'

Gabe raises his eyebrows in anticipation.

'Fingerprints were found on the image. They weren't easy to get, as paper can be tricky at the best of times. Anyway, we got two sets. A right thumb and index plus another full set, these matched with the prints we took from you on Saturday, Margot. But we also got partial prints of a left thumb and index finger that didn't match yours.'

'So you can work out who it is?' I say.

'I'll get to that. The image was actually printed on the back of a power bill.'

'A power bill?'

'It's the final sheet. Sometimes it's sent with the rest of the bill but there's nothing to identify who received it. There was an Energy Australia logo at the bottom of the page, and we could trawl the millions of people on the Energy Australia database to find who might live nearby, but that's unlikely to be useful, given about a third of the state uses Energy Australia and we have to keep the radius of the search open.'

'So you've got fingerprints, but what about foot prints or the bottle?' Gabe says.

'We've found size-twelve boot prints near the property, which will help with eliminating potential suspects, but short of knocking on every door of every man with big feet in the city, that information alone won't help a great deal. The bottle, Chivas Regal, was smashed and charred. There's nothing usable in terms of identification there.'

'Right.'

'The prints on the image is our best lead at the moment. The second set we assume must belong to the person who placed it there. I know you're convinced you're the only person who touched it, Margot, but we will take your prints, Gabe, just to eliminate you.'

'I'm assuming you've already run the prints through a database?' he says.

'When we ran the prints nothing came back, so he's not on the system and even if we got a match it would mean we had a suspect for the image, but it's also possible the two are not linked, the fire and the image.'

'Possible,' Gabe said. 'But extraordinarily unlikely, surely?'

'There's room for doubt. We got a good sample so if they do anything else, if they commit any other crime and leave a left thumb or left index print, we'll be able to connect the two.'

It might be a criminal who has gotten lucky, an arsonist who has never been caught. A mind that's burning, itching to cause carnage. Or, since the prints don't match any other crime or criminal, maybe this was a first offence. A first-time crim. I can't think which is worse – a hardened criminal who's evaded authorities or someone who hated us so much they're prepared to become one.

'There was something else,' Simms says. 'The station officer reported that the nature of the fire suggests most of the fuel used was not in close proximity to the incendiary device.'

'In plain language that means—'

'Most of the fuel was in the lounge room, not the study where the Molotov cocktail landed. So someone has likely spread fuel in the house before throwing the Molotov cocktail through the window. I'm waiting on the full report from the fire investigation unit, but it could be that the door was left open to accelerate the fire by providing more oxygen, or someone simply forgot to close it.'

'You're joking,' Gabe says.

'Wish I was. It means someone was inside your house.'

I feel goosebumps rise in my forearms. Gabe's arm comes around my shoulders. 'But why wouldn't they light it from inside silently? Why would they bother breaking the window and waking us up?'

His shoulders rise and he turns his palms to us. 'That's a question I'm afraid I can't answer.'

•

In the early afternoon on Monday I have Xanthe. She smiles politely.

'Come on through.' With some clients, I must read over their notes before each visit to refresh my mind; some patients I see only once a month and it's necessary to rehash the previous visits. But not with Xanthe as she comes twice a week.

She falls into the seat, and her head bobbles a little. She's clearly back on her medication. Or rather she's on *something*. Her pupils are a little dilated, though her hands are steady. I'm reminded of my suspicions about Xanthe's reported fear of mirrors. She wears make-up perfectly applied, which would be impossible for her to do herself if her spectrophobia was genuine and she couldn't look in the mirror. It's possible someone else put it on, of course, but with her sooty lashes and gently contoured cheeks it's another small inconsistency. This is the problem with a pathological liar: it's impossible to know what's true and what's a fantasy. That doesn't mean she isn't unwell; it's just hard to know precisely what she's struggling with.

'I'm feeling better,' she says. She scratches at her hairline and I see a faint bruise on the inside of her wrist. No real evidence of abuse, but it's concerning.

'How are things with Jacob?'

'They're good. We've been better lately.'

'And you've been taking your medication?'

She gives an enthusiastic nod. 'Yeah, every day. Jacob's been making me take it. He's been saying it makes me more stable.'

'How did you feel when he said that?'

'I felt good. It means the medication is good for me. It makes me easier to be around.' She glances about absently as if she was in the process of doing something and she's forgotten what it was.

'I'm glad you're taking your medication again, Xanthe.' Her gaze comes back to me. 'Do you think it's healthy that Jacob has set that as a condition of your relationship, that you are medicated?'

Lips pout, eyes roll. She's uncertain, almost sad. 'I think if he's happy, I'm happy. I don't like to upset him, you know?'

Poor thing, I think. A case study of dependence. Her happiness isn't contingent on his happiness, only on his *presence*. It doesn't sound like co-dependency, because he doesn't appear to need her. She's just convenient for him.

'What happens when you upset him?'

She averts her gaze, touches her ear. 'Well nothing, really. It's not nice to upset the people you love.'

'So you love him?'

'I think I do,' she says. 'I must love him, right?'

'Why?'

She looks ashamed, averts her gaze to the window, the world outside. 'He's all I've got.'

I feel like I haven't made any progress with her in so long. She still cuts, she still lies, she still maintains unhealthy habits and relationships. Now she thinks she loves this boyfriend.

'You don't love someone just because you're in a relationship, Xanthe.'

'You have to love your family though,' she says.

'Your family? What do you mean? Do you see Jacob as family?'

She looks guilty for a second, her eyes moving to the window. She doesn't answer the question. 'I am less paranoid now, too. That's something else that's been better.'

I make a note. *Sees Jacob as family.* 'I didn't know you felt paranoid.'

'Sometimes. Like earlier this week. I was convinced someone was following me.'

I swallow the hard knot that forms in my throat and before I can ask a question she is speaking again.

'Crazy, right? Jacob said it was my paranoia. He says that no one would follow me all the way home.'

'Home from where?'

'Oh, from here. I thought a white car was following me. I was in an Uber. But then when I got out and went to my front door they drove past.'

Curious, I think. Two patients have similar stories. And *I* was followed by a white Toyota. It happened the night of the fire. It has to be a coincidence, but . . . what if it's not?

'Xanthe, just to be on the safe side, if you ever feel like someone is following you, assume that it's possibly true. Try get an image of them in your mind, remember the number plate, report it to the police.' Her eyes are suddenly wide with panic. The room is still and breathless for a moment.

This is clearly a breach of protocol; I'm not viewing her case in isolation. All signs point to paranoia, and I can't let her leave believing someone dangerous might be stalking her. I've spent so long trying to convince her that her problems are in her head and now I'm telling her they might be out here in the real world, tangible, sharp-toothed things with real consequences.

'That's only to keep you safe,' I say. 'It's very, very unlikely you are being followed at all.'

NINE

OUTSIDE THE CAFE, long-dead leaves line the gutter and the sidewalk is busy with foot traffic. Inside, it's all Saturday morning regulars, exercise attire aplenty, with the local mums who've walked the Tan before meeting up for their morning latte. The coffee maker shrieks as the barista steams milk. It's the usual barista, good-looking, green eyes, dark hair.

She raises her eyebrows at me as I pass. I find a quiet seat in the far corner, waiting until Linda arrives. She's a bubbly school friend, always ready for a drink, a better talker than listener, but I don't mind. She was the first to offer us a place to stay when she heard about the fire. We sit there in the corner. Linda tells me about her new man. *Ricardo.*

'Sounds exotic,' I say.

'He's not really. He grew up in Footscray, which I guess is a little exotic to some.'

'No Porsche this time, then?'

'No, sadly. He's younger than me though.'

I tune out for a moment and find my gaze resting on the recognisable shape of a man. A man I know. *Cormac. This* is his cafe. He works at Black Bean. *Shit.* He picks up two coffees from the barista, carrying them to a table. I've not seen him like this, hair tousled, pinned on one side behind his ear by a pen. Black jeans and a tight black t-shirt, so you can see the contours of his chest. It does happen, seeing clients outside of a clinical setting – supermarkets, the park, school pick-up: you never know where they might turn up. But this feels different somehow. I'm at his place of work. He smiles as he sets two coffees on a table for a couple. I watch as the woman's gaze lingers on Cormac as he strides back towards the barista. We have a different waiter. We didn't get Cormac, thankfully.

I feel something touch the back of my hand. I snap back to focus on Linda and see she has placed a napkin on my wrist.

'What's this for?'

'To mop up the drool,' she says.

I can feel my cheeks glowing. 'No, I know him,' I say, embarrassed.

'You do? How?'

A wrong step: I shouldn't have acknowledged I know him at all. I don't speak for a moment. I just tilt my head a little and eye her.

She figures it out. Her mouth opens. 'He's a client of yours.'

'No,' I say. 'I'm not saying that.'

She licks her lips. 'He looks pretty normal to me.'

'Mental health issues happen to everyone, including exceptionally good-looking young men. In fact,' I add, 'young men are one of the highest risk groups for mental illness, because they don't ask for help.'

'Well, you can let him know if I can help in any way, I'm more than happy to.'

'Bit young for you,' I tease.

When our coffees come, two trim lattes, the waitress puts mine down and I find the foam is shaped in a heart. I take a quick sip before Linda notices. Coincidence, I'm sure. I glance towards the barista. She's busy; the lunch rush is gearing up into full swing.

We chat for a while, then Linda says, 'Well, are you going to call your friend over for an introduction?'

I stare down at the coffee foam clinging to the interior of my cup. This entire situation is making me uncomfortable. Linda would never deliberately do anything to jeopardise my career, but she is careless, and you never know who might be listening. 'I'd love to help with this midlife promiscuity, but obviously I can't,' I say, finally meeting her gaze.

'Spoilsport.'

After our coffees, Linda gets up to leave.

'I'm going to stay on for a bit. Gabe is meeting me,' I say.

'Right,' she says, with a not-too-subtle wink. She air-kisses my cheek, turns to find Cormac with her eyes and says, 'Enjoy.'

I sit there, keeping my head down, eyes averted. I turn my phone to silent, so it won't ring and catch his attention. A couple sits on the table next to me, and they begin dismantling a newspaper, talking quietly between themselves. I order one more coffee and follow Cormac with my eyes.

I'm there for an hour. The lunch crowd comes and goes and I stay looking down at my phone, stealing occasional glances as the afternoon wears on. Out on the street I see rain starting to fall. I know I should leave before I end up the only one left, and Cormac will inevitably notice his psychologist sitting alone. There are four waitstaff and fortunately he's not working any of the tables near me. He stands beside the coffee machine now, flirting with the barista, who touches his arm when she laughs. *He made her laugh.* The barista with the green eyes. He disappears through a door to the kitchen and comes back with his backpack on.

He steps close to her. I see it and my heart seems to cease beating for a second. A kiss. Not on the cheek but on the lips. It's a tiny, uncomfortable moment for me. I interrogate the feeling: why do I care? Why am I still sitting here, stalking a client?

I try to answer these questions, I try to understand my motivations, but I can't. They kissed, the beautiful young woman behind the coffee machine and Cormac. Perhaps this woman can make him happy. Perhaps he won't need our sessions if he has her.

Then he leaves. I rise, quickly forcing a twenty dollar note into the waitress's hand and don't wait for the change. I step past a couple, who stand in the entrance collapsing rain-slicked umbrellas. Then I'm outside. He's just ahead, conjuring his own umbrella from somewhere. He strides quickly, pushing headphones into his ears and touching his phone. He's talking to someone.

What are you doing, Margot?

The rain continues to fall, soaking the shoulders of my blouse. The urge to follow him is so strange and sudden, I don't know where it's come from. I want to understand him more, I tell myself, to help treat him.

I go back and get in my car, turn the heating on and set off. New buds of rain sprout on the glass between each swish of the wipers.

I get home and Gabe is there, studying me from the kitchen bench. I can barely meet his eyes, with shame crawling below my skin like cockroaches. Is this *emotional* cheating? I was almost jealous, protective of another man. I cared and was hurt. I didn't think about how Gabe would react until now. 'Long brunch,' he says.

'Yeah, you know Linda, couldn't shut her up.'

'Boozy?'

'No,' I say, trying to smile.

'That's funny,' he says. 'I bumped into Linda half an hour ago at the grocer. She got a little flustered when I asked her what time she left brunch. She said both ten minutes ago and an hour ago. Then she asked me if I was meeting you.'

I drop my bag on the bench, chew my lips. 'I'm stressed. All I wanted was some alone time,' I say. 'I got reading the newspaper.'

I pull my phone out and see four missed calls from Gabe. 'I've only now seen the calls, sorry.' My phone was on silent.

'I'm stressed about the house, too, Margot, but it's been hours.'

'I said I'm sorry.' It comes out sharp, antagonistic.

He looks deep into my eyes now. 'Can you please communicate in the future?'

'I will,' I say, then try to change the subject. 'How was your day?'

'It was fine. I met July's boyfriend.'

'Where?'

'He dropped her home. I guess they were studying together today. Nice kid. A little preppy.'

'What do you mean?'

'He reeks of private school privilege, but not in a bad way. Too polite, too groomed. You know?'

'Sure. I think we need to talk to her about being cautious outside of the house right now.'

He stands from his stool and goes in behind the bench. The downlights shadow his eyes. 'Cautious how?'

I lean over the kitchen bench and reach into the cupboard for a wine glass. 'Someone tried to burn our house down. She needs to keep us informed about where she is at all times, and who with. She can't come and go as she pleases.' *Rich coming from me, ignoring calls all day,* I think. 'Can you pass me the wine?'

'I agree, but she's seventeen, Margot,' he says, pulling a bottle of pinot noir from the wine rack. 'She's going to have her own life. We already told her once that she needs to keep us in the loop.'

He's right.

'Corkscrew please.'

Gabe opens four drawers before he finally produces it. I let out a small huff of laughter.

'So hard to find anything in this house,' he says.

I open the bottle of wine then look at the clock and see it is only three. Still I pour myself a glass, take a sip, then say, 'July will understand if we have to enforce a curfew, I'll talk to her again. I don't mind her spending time with Hudson, but I'd rather they do it here where she's safe.'

'You're the boss.'

TEN

JOE RUBS HIS left eye with his knuckles. He sniffs and huffs. It could be his work, finally getting to him. I saw one image of death and it has stayed with me. It's visited me when I'm in bed waiting for sleep, the explosion of flesh and blood.

I know the image was likely downloaded but I can't help thinking about the gnawing possibility that the person who printed it is the person who photographed it.

'So, how are things at work, Joe?'

He glances up suddenly, as if surprised. 'Oh, fine.'

'You seem a little down today,' I add.

He smiles but there is no joy in it. 'Do I?'

'You do. Is there something going on at home?'

He shifts his hips deeper into the seat. 'No. The usual.'

'So no changes? Have you been sleeping well?'

'Yeah, sort of. I mean there's been a couple of bad nights.'

'So not a full night every night?'

'No. I've been drinking a little. I heard that affects sleep. Maybe that's why I'm so tired.'

'Do you think it would be a good idea to work out why you're drinking more? I'm assuming it has gotten more frequent?'

'You could say that. I've been drinking a nightcap of scotch to help me sleep.'

'Every second night? Every night? Twice a week?'

'Most nights, actually, especially Thursday, Friday, Saturday. My wife wants me to start going with her to mass again but I'm always so tired,' he says. It chills me. He's self-medicating, he's clearly not well. His eyes fix on my pen. 'That's a Mont Blanc.'

I look down and smile, as if noticing it for the first time. 'It is. Well spotted.'

'Expensive.'

'I wouldn't know, it was a gift.'

'Lucky girl,' he says.

I push the conversation back on track. 'Are you doing anything else to help with your sleep?'

His eyes rise from the pen to mine. 'Like what?'

'Putting your phone away earlier?'

'Yeah, I'm not playing so many games. I'm trying to find other ways to entertain myself.'

'What other ways?'

I see his Adam's apple move up and down. I study the explosions of tiny red veins in his cheeks, at the tip of his nose. Is he blushing? 'Well I'm trying to read books, like you said. I started one called *Dark Tide*. It's quite good.'

'Yeah, what's it about?'

'A backpacker who disappeared in New Zealand. It's a true crime one.'

'Right. Do you feel you could read before bed to help you sleep instead of having a drink?'

'Maybe,' he says. 'But I like a drink. I do both.'

'Well, do you know how we define problematic drinking?'

'If I can't stop?' he asks.

'Yeah, that is one way. That's called dependency, which is problematic. Another way of putting it would be if you feel like you can't control it. But it sounds to me like you're in control for now.'

'I don't want to lose control,' he says, and there's something about the way he says it with a little sadness that gives me pause. 'I worry sometimes that I'm a bad person.'

'How so?'

'Well, how I treat my wife. We argue, but it's always worse after I've had a couple of drams of Chivas.'

Something slaps me, almost knocking me off my seat. *Chivas.* That was the bottle used for the Molotov cocktail. I try to keep my face neutral, stalling for a moment by taking a sip of my water. Joe would have endless access to graphic images. It's possible I'm looking into the eyes of the man who almost killed me and my family. But why? It doesn't make sense. 'Margot?' The sound of my name shakes me out of my trance.

'Sorry,' I say, smiling. 'All couples have arguments. That doesn't make you a bad person. Is there anything else?'

'Well little things, like when I found that phone on the train.'

'You gave it back, though. That doesn't make you bad.'

'No, but I was tempted to keep it. Or to try to unlock it to see the messages and photos. I didn't think to hand it in until they called. And my drinking . . . I spend too much on whisky.'

I can feel the heat in my limbs. I've got to act normal. I can't let him know I'm suspicious. I find my eyes roaming the carpet, coming to rest on his shoes. They're bigger than Gabe's and Gabe is a size ten. 'So has your drinking affected your work in any way?'

'No,' he says. 'Work's been fine. I was late last Thursday but only because my train was running behind schedule.'

Last Thursday. The fire was Wednesday. What if he missed the early train because he overslept from a late night? I need to be careful – I can't just call the police with a suspicion. And it's a breach of confidentiality. If I get this wrong it would ruin my career. What if he did do it, though? What if he still wants to hurt me? I feel heat under my arms, in my lower back. I eye the clock. Five more minutes. Five minutes to get through. I keep scribbling on my pad, talking to him, asking him questions, and when the time comes, I stand aside to let him go out the door. He pauses close to me.

'When am I in next?' he says.

'Same time in a fortnight.' *Can you hear my heart pounding?* I wonder.

'Looking forward to it,' he says, before striding from the room. I follow him to the side door, my eyes staying with him as he opens it and steps out into the alleyway.

'Anna,' I say, moving behind the reception desk, leaning in close to her so the waiting client doesn't hear.

'Yes, Margot.'

'Can you do me a favour and discreetly follow Joe to his car?'

'Now?'

'Yes, now. He's just left,' I say quietly but perhaps a little too firmly, because when she stands her seat falls back, clattering against the floorboards. 'Please find out the make and colour of his car. Stroll past like you're getting a coffee.' I turn back to my next client. 'Sorry,' I say, louder now. 'Come on through, Willow.'

She looks up from her phone, offers me a sad smile then rises, following me into my office. Willow's father was caught messaging one of her schoolfriends a couple of years ago and she hasn't been right since. We talk for an hour but I can't concentrate. I find my mind wandering back to my previous session with Joe. I make notes and ask questions, trying to focus on Willow, but the moment the session ends and she leaves I find myself striding towards the lobby, butterflies beating hard in my chest. Anna looks up, indifferent. She holds a yellow Post-it note out towards me. Written on it are two words. One is "White", the other is "Toyota". *It's him.*

ELEVEN

I CALL AN old mentor, Paul, who has always helped me with difficult clients. He's been a psychologist for almost forty years. I explain the situation to him. 'My advice would be to drop the client. Termination on grounds of a conflict of interest. Make a note that he reminds you too much of someone, and pass him on. Enhance security at your practice.' It sounds easy enough, but I know it's not so straightforward. Since Peter I've not broken a single rule; I've always followed protocol to a fault. But I'm skating on thin ice.

'Is that . . . possibly malpractice? He's not vulnerable but I have a duty—'

'You have a genuine concern and no medical board could ever prove that you don't have a conflict of interest. Or perhaps declare some countertransference you can't overcome. Say he reminds you of a bad ex.'

'Alright,' I say. 'And could I involve the police?'

'On what you've told me, I would say no. Psychologists *do* have an obligation to report clients to the authorities if there is a credible risk of harm to a patient or anyone else. *Credible* being the operative word. Drinking whisky and having big feet isn't proof.

Likewise driving the most common car on the road. None of this is entirely credible even if you yourself are convinced. You can speak in general terms to a cop you know and trust, seek advice from them but you cannot in any way identify the client unless you have something concrete.'

After the call, I sit at my desk and dial the cop's number.

'Simms,' he answers.

'Hi it's Margot Scott here,' I say, feeling a little uncertain.

'Yes, hi Margot.'

'I'm in a bit of a situation.'

I hear a door close. 'Go on.'

'Well I don't know how to say this, but I think I have a suspect for the arson.'

'Right, when you say you *have* a suspect—'

'Not with me – I mean I can't really say who it is.'

'A client then?' I wince. 'What makes you think this individual is involved?'

'Well, I was followed by the same make and colour car the night it happened that this person drives. And this person drinks the brand of whisky that was used for the Molotov cocktail. Plus their work.'

'What does he do?'

'Well I didn't say it was a *he* and I can't actually say what they do. That would be a breach of confidentiality.'

'Right, well, unless he sets fire for a living I don't know how that would be relevant.' I realise that Simms is convinced it was a man, which suggests they've made some progress on the case, or maybe it's the simple fact of the size-twelve boot prints.

'He has access to loads of obscene images like the one that was left behind, that's all I can say.'

'A moderator of some sort?'

I have a sinking feeling. This conversation isn't going how I thought. I just wanted advice. 'I can't say yes.'

'But it's a yes, I get it. It's compelling, but totally circumstantial.'

'Look, I'm just worried about him. I can't give you any more information. I just want advice.'

He clears his throat. 'Well I understand you're in a tough spot, but we are working hard, making progress. Continue to be vigilant and I'll get in touch with you as soon as we have anything at all. You'll likely see suspicious things everywhere you look; that's what happens after crimes. You can feel paranoid and shaken up. It might be worth getting therapy yourself and leaving the investigating up to us.'

I'm taken aback. I've never needed counselling myself; I bite my tongue and think for a second. If I had something that proved it, something that removed the doubt, then confidentiality wouldn't be an issue at all. 'Right, well, I'll leave it with you.'

'And to give you peace of mind I'll make sure we take a closer look at *everyone* coming and going from your place of work,' he says.

'Thanks,' I say, before hanging up. I gently tap my phone to my forehead. I don't like this, I think. I don't like this at all.

•

Cormac enters the practice. His stubble is a little shorter, tidier and his cheeks are red as though he's run here.

'Made it just in time. I got held up at work.'

'That's fine. Come through.'

I lead him to my room and he does his usual routine, eyeing my bookshelf, running his hand along the spines, before settling into his seat.

I fill both the glasses of water before placing my pad on my lap and glancing over my notes. 'In our last session we were talking about when you arrived in Australia. How hard it was to adjust.'

'We came over when I was young, not long after what happened with my dad. Mum was sort of broken, you know. She was vacant, I can see it now. Stressed, no money, two kids. It would have been hell for her. It wasn't long until she started to dabble more in drugs. After what Dad did, it's hard to blame her.' I flick back to a previous note from our first session. *Doesn't blame his father; blames outsiders like the mistress.*

'It's not uncommon for people to self-medicate when they have young children and no support network.' I can't help but think about the glass of wine I've been having most nights this week.

'That's it, no support network. It wasn't the move, it was the fact Dad was gone. He was a bastard to her, but sometimes I wonder if she didn't regret it all, trying to leave him in the first place and taking us kids.'

'So you think she is somehow responsible herself?'

'No, I don't know. She let us down when she got here, and it's hard to look past that. Anyway, we arrived. I was bullied a little for my accent, but an Irish accent is a stubborn mule. When it's there it's not easy to get rid of. My sister copped it as bad. She was bullied, too, but girl bullying is different. Girls can break each other down psychologically, leaving scars that stay for years. My sister is seventeen now and she's still messed up from everything. Even more than me.'

'Let's circle back to that later, Cormac,' I say, glancing at the clock, changing tack. 'Maybe for now you could tell me about any other changes in your life lately. How is work?'

'Work?' he says. 'Well, it's good. It's great actually. My personal life is fine, other than I've had a dodgy bastard hanging out in the alley behind our flat.'

'That's not good,' I say. I want to know about the girl, his relationship. I want to know why he hasn't mentioned her. 'So are you making friends through your new job?' I give a small smile.

'Don't,' he says, with a rueful grin.

'Don't what?'

'Don't you do that smile, don't you dare.'

I find my smile growing now. I try to swallow it, push it away, but I can't. 'What smile? I just want to know if you're making friends, that's all.'

'Oh, you have a way about you, don't you? One look and you can suck the thoughts right out of my head. One look and you could do anything to—'

I raise my palm. 'That's not appropriate, Cormac,' I say, ripping that line of conversation up by the roots.

'Alright, alright,' he says. 'I'm sorry, I can't help myself. Well, to answer your question, I did meet a girl, actually. The barista and me are in the middle of a fling, I guess you would call it.'

'A fling?'

'A fling, yes. She's falling pretty hard for your boy.'

'And you? How do you feel about her?'

'It's not her I want,' he says. His eyes are boring into mine. That smile, all lips, dimples, shining eyes. I think about Peter, about how close I let him get and how it ended. Then I think about Gabe and my family and my career and that sinking feeling I had when I called Simms comes back. I don't want to lose control of the situation with any of my clients, not Joe, not Cormac.

'So,' I continue, ignoring the implication of his words, 'you're leading her on?'

'Am I like your other clients, Margot?' He asks, ignoring my question.

I take a sip of my water, swallow hard, shift in my seat to pull my dress a little lower. 'We're not here to talk about my *other* clients, Cormac, we are here to talk about you.' I place my pen on the page, then meet his eyes again. 'Let's go back a bit here. Tell me more about this man in the alleyway. Are you concerned it's the same man you told me about last time, the man that followed you home?'

'I'm not sure. I doubt he's the same person. I just figured the guy who followed me was a pervert or something. I wasn't worried. I can handle myself.'

'I'm sure you can. Where did he follow you from?'

'Well from near here.' My intestines curl into knots. *Joe.*

'I didn't notice at first,' he continues, 'but he was there every time I looked up until I got home.'

'What did he look like?'

'Normal enough. Forties. Bald. Can't remember what he was wearing.'

•

That evening I get back to the house we're renting and find July and Gabe watching TV in the lounge.

'Where's Evan?' I ask, putting my bag down on the table.

'He's up in his room,' July says. 'Been up there for hours.'

Gabe bought him a new computer this morning, another thing I hope the insurance will cover. *As long as it's the same model so they can't deny the claim,* Gabe had promised. 'Is he gaming?'

July turns back to me and shrugs. I see pots boiling away on the stove.

I climb the stairs and knock on his door. There is no response, just silence on the other side of the door. 'Evan?' I call.

A few more seconds, then I knock harder. 'Evan, I'm coming in.'

I push the door open. The curtains are closed. I scan the dark of the room. I can see he has put up a poster on the wall to make it feel more like home and his computer is all set up in the corner. Then I see a shape in the bed.

'Evan?' I say. 'What's happening here?'

It looks like he is sleeping, the brown curls of hair against the pillow, the points of his bony frame shaping the peaks of the blanket. Then I realise he is moving, but not with normal breathing: more of a shivering. I reach out for his shoulder pulling gently, but he doesn't turn towards me.

'Evan?'

'Go away,' he mutters, with tears in his voice.

'What is it? What's wrong?'

He lets me pull him, gently turning him. In the glow of the streetlight coming through the curtains I can see the shine on his cheeks. I feel anxious more than sad. He's never like this; something has gotten to him.

'Evan, tell me what's wrong?'

'I can't,' he says.

'It doesn't matter what it is, Evan, I can help you.' I imagine all the things that could have gone wrong. My boy is too delicate to have done anything that would warrant this sort of response, too young to join a gang, or have a pregnant girlfriend. But everything is so much bigger in your head at that age. 'Evan, you're going to tell me why you are upset, and we are going to work it out together.'

'It's my fault,' he says.

'What's your fault?'

'The fire.' The tears are clearing now, but his voice still trembles.

'Nonsense. Someone pitched a bottle through our window. How is it your fault?'

'It was Raze.'

'Raze?' I say. I've heard the name before.

He pulls himself up, sitting against the headboard. I reach for the bedside lamp, turn it on and he squints against the light.

Last time we banned him from his computer for a week he was teasing another gamer online. 'Evan, you've not been bullying that kid online again have you?'

'No, he's just another player.' It's all I can do to keep from rolling my eyes. 'He made the others in my clan kick me out and he took my place. That's why I joined another clan.'

I draw a long breath, assessing the situation. I can't tell him that this is all frivolous, that the real world is outside, that the internet is intangible, irrelevant to life, because it's not true; the cyber sphere is as much a part of the real world as anything else. But still I feel frustrated.

'So Raze kicked you out? How does that make you responsible for the fire?'

I think about the word, *Raze*, to level or destroy. It's a coincidence, surely. Evan's gaming alias is probably *Destroyer* or *Hell bringer*.

'When I joined another clan, he told me to quit or he would dox me. But I didn't quit. Then he said he knows where I live. He said he was going to swat me.'

I have no idea what any of these words mean, but they don't sound particularly threatening.

'What is dox and swat?'

He sniffs, tilts his head forward. 'Dox is to reveal someone's real identity and personal details online. I stream, so people can see my screen and my face, but that's it, nothing else.'

'How would he do that?'

'Hacking, usually, or there are other ways. By tracking my IP address he would know our suburb, then using screengrabs from my streams and trying to match my face to photos on other people's Facebook and Instagram pages, especially tagged at local places like restaurants or parks.' He's talking about my social media accounts and July's. Not Gabe's, I note, because Gabe is absent from the online world. The only information you will find there is his short profile on the webpage for Moore and Wansbone Accountants. You're much more likely to find Gabe reading a book or a newspaper then staring at his phone.

'What do you mean by "Swatting"?'

'Swatting is when people call in a serious crime to a police department and they give them another gamer's address. Then police storm their house and it often comes up on live streams. I was worried that would happen, but then what happened was worse.'

'Oh, Evan, I doubt that's the case here. Raze, whoever he is, probably lives in another country.'

'He doesn't, he lives here. He told me he lives in Melbourne. I *know* he lives in Melbourne.'

'How could you possibly know that?'

'I just do,' he says.

'Still, that doesn't prove anything.'

'I've been careful since then, always using a proxy server to hide my location. I have location services disabled on my phone and computer. I make sure there is nothing behind me when I'm streaming.'

'That's good to hear, that you're being careful. Like I said, I'm sure it's a coincidence.' *Although there have been far too many of those lately.*

'There was something else,' he says.

'What?'

He gets out of bed and crosses the room to his computer monitor, switching it on. I see the dark tones of the gaming profile, an image of Evan's character, a herculean figure with bare chest, a long rifle slung over his shoulder. He clicks the direct messages tab and my stomach falls through the floor.

Next time u wont escape ;)

TWELVE

'EVAN,' I SAY, TRYING to keep my voice calm. 'This doesn't mean anything. Even if it's true, it doesn't mean it's your fault. The fire was in the news. He could have seen it there, or maybe he meant you won't escape on the game?'

I'm suddenly angry at July for posting the image on her Instagram and Snapchat. He folds his arms, but neither of us turns away from the screen. 'He's a pyscho, Mum.'

'Maybe, but we're safe now.'

I see other messages in his inbox. Messages Evan has sent.

We're going to rape you

KYS loser

'Evan, did you send those messages?'

Despite the dark of the room I see his cheeks flush.

'Tell me.'

'Everyone talks like that online.'

'We've been through this. This better not be the same kid you were bullying with your friends before?'

He just shrugs, which gives me the answer. No wonder he feels guilty.

'It's just how people talk in gaming, it doesn't matter.'

'That doesn't make it right. What does KYS mean?'

'It's just something people say.'

My voice rises. 'What does it mean?'

'Kill yourself.'

My anger boils over. 'Are you insane, Evan? What the hell is wrong with you? Never send that to anyone ever again. Do you understand me?'

He nods. 'I'm sorry, Mum. People send worse stuff all the time. People say they hope I get cancer, or they're going to throw acid in my face.'

'You're not sorry, or you wouldn't have done it again. Wasn't it enough we banned you last time? Do we need to take all your gaming away?'

'No, I won't do it anymore.'

Kill yourself. I think about the words again. What would happen if someone actually did kill themselves? How would it affect my son? 'And you sent these messages to this Raze? You provoked him? How could *anyone* tell someone else to kill themselves? I expected so much better from you.'

'He started it.'

'I don't care if he started it. You walk away, you block him. Have you been streaming yourself since we started staying at this house?'

'No.'

'Did he definitely know our address before? Did he tell you?'

He turns away from the computer, his eyes finding the ceiling as he thinks. 'No, he never said our actual address, he just said he knew it. He said we had a big weatherboard house.'

'That's how I would describe eighty percent of homes in the South East of the city.' I reach for the mouse. 'How do I log off? How do I block him?'

'If he's good, he would have worked out the IP already, but that doesn't mean he has the address, probably just the suburb and ISP.'

'So it's easy to do?'

'Easy enough.'

'Have you done it to him?'

He looks guilty in the screen light. 'I have his IP, too. Well, he uses a couple of different ones, but I know sometimes he is down near Pakenham somewhere and sometimes he is near the CBD.'

Pakenham. I know Joe lives close to the city but maybe he also has a house down there. 'I'm going to call the police.'

'No,' he says. 'Please, Mum, don't make him angry.'

Don't make him angry. 'Have you seen him angry before?'

'Last time he spammed me with images. The most messed up images on the net.'

Joe. I lower myself onto Evan's bed, the possibilities flying through my mind. *I'm up late playing games,* Joe had said. I assumed he meant games on his phone, but what if he meant the games Evan plays? What if Joe didn't even know I lived there? Or worse, what if Joe started seeing me to be closer to Evan, knowing I was Evan's mum. Now that I think about it, I have never verified that Joe works for Rad. He pays for his own sessions and is supposedly reimbursed by the company. Everything I know about him, he has told me. Other patients reported being followed – is it a coincidence or perhaps Joe really is sick; perhaps he's a voyeur who got bored, who wanted to make his own drama.

'It's a coincidence, Evan,' I say. 'If you're right and this person is involved, the police will find him, but that would mean it is *his* fault and *not* yours. You understand that, right?'

He nods.

'Good. In the future don't be so stupid as to provoke these sickos,' I say. 'Now I want you to come downstairs when you're ready and spend some time with us. Dinner will be ready soon.'

But at the table, I can barely concentrate on my food. Evan doesn't eat much either. He's worried sick.

After dinner, when the kids are on the couch in front of the TV, I decide I can't wait any longer to talk to Gabe. I approach him as he's doing the dishes. He's just dried a pot and is opening drawers trying to figure out where it came from. I touch his shoulder and when he turns back, I point up and nod towards the stairs.

He takes the tea towel from over his shoulder and tosses it on the bench, then follows me out of the open kitchen-lounge area up into our bedroom.

'What is it?' he says, closing the door behind him.

'It's about the fire. Evan is worried it was one of his gaming friends,' I begin. I explain the situation, the message Evan received.

'He was crying real tears?'

'Yes, real tears. He's obviously shaken up, carrying around this guilt for the past week.'

'Shit, that's a heavy load for a kid to bear in silence. No wonder he broke down.'

'It's not just that,' I say. 'There's a client I'm seeing. He's a gamer, he drives a white Toyota, he drinks Chivas Regal and sees any number of disturbing images every day in his job.'

I can see his jaw working, chewing on this new information. His head tilts a few degrees, suggesting he's sceptical.

'And you think it might be this guy, this client?'

'Well, I'm convinced, actually. I spoke to Simms.'

The scepticism slides from his face, replaced instantly by frustration. 'Do you think that might be just a *little* irresponsible, Margot?' He manages to keep his voice even.

'Irresponsible? I'm protecting *our* family. I only asked for advice, I didn't identify the client.'

He blows his cheeks out. 'I just wish you had talked to me about it first. I don't think you should be taking any risks over a suspicion.'

I think about Joe's words. His dreams of hurting someone with a fire extinguisher, his drinking, the fact he could rationalise potential violence. But I know I can't tell Gabe this. He's a stickler for confidentiality. When we were first dating I was dragged through a tribunal. It was early in my career, after Peter. Because of Peter's wealthy ex-girlfriend the story was in the media. I've been thinking about him so much more lately. I remember that day like it all happened this morning. Suddenly I'm back there racing towards him, telling myself that no one would blame me, holding my breath, flooring the car to beat a red light. The ringing was like a heartbeat. The ringing was all I had. Finally he answered, the voice instantly conjuring the man in my mind. Tall, thin, a tangle of dark hair, a little gaunt yet somehow still very handsome.

'Peter, it's Margot. I'm on my way.'

'You're coming now?' Peter said, his voice narcotically slow and calm.

'I am, yes. The police called me.' I paused, gathered my thoughts. 'I want you to know that I'm with you, do you understand? We can get you through this.' I swerved out of my lane to pass a taxi. A horn blared. My palm ached, clutching the wheel.

'Where are you?'

'I'm in my car right now, driving to your apartment. No one is going to blame you for this, no one is going to lock you up.'

'I can't. I—' A heavy pause, and I wondered what he might have taken. Doctors had a habit of over-prescribing sedatives, SSRIs, sleep aids; his bathroom cupboard was a pharmacy.

'What? Peter? You can't what?'

'I can't continue with this. I can't. You lied to me, Margot.'

'Peter. You have value. You are loved.' I didn't want to mention his family but I had to. 'You have a child.' *And an ex-girlfriend who is pregnant,* I could have added. 'You have a father and a mother who both love you.'

'They're going to lock me away. You're working with them. It's never been about me, has it? I love—.'

'—No,' I cut him off. 'No, Peter. This isn't about me. This is about you. You can't depend on me to feel happy and calm. But I'm here to help. I promised you and I keep my promises to patients.'

'*Patients*,' he said.

I might as well have said customers. 'You know what I mean – the people I see.' I was thinking of how to keep him on the line, keep him talking, when he spoke again.

'You did this to me, Margot. You did this.'

The line cut out as I got close. I checked my phone to make sure the call was recorded then I rang him again, but it went straight to voicemail. He'd turned the phone off.

'Well,' Gabe says, snapping me back to the moment. 'What can we do?'

'If you knew some of the things this person told me, Gabe, some of the clues – then you would understand. The police are looking at anyone visiting the clinic, so hopefully they will check him out.'

He lowers himself onto the edge of the bed and folds his arms. 'Okay, well I just hope you know what you're doing.'

'I have an obligation to report serious crimes to the police, but only if I believe that a client's confession is credible. I know I shouldn't speculate, but all the evidence is pointing to this person.'

'Say it is this guy. What if he knows where we're staying?'

'I've been paying attention. Even if this Raze is my client and he has the IP address here, it doesn't mean he has the street address.'

I move closer to him, standing before him on the edge of the bed. I rub his upper arms. He softens, unfolds his arms and wraps them around the tops of my legs.

'Look, I'm sorry if I'm stressed. It's just an awful position to be in. Part of me was hoping it all was truly random, you know. Part of me was hoping it would just disappear, but if someone has cause to do it once then what would stop them doing it again?' he asks.

It's a question I can't answer. 'We've just got to be careful. I don't know what more we can do.'

His grip on my upper legs loosens and I step back to read his expression. He's staring at the carpet at my feet, chewing his lip. 'What're the rules with an anonymous tip?'

'What?'

'Well, what if the police received an anonymous tip? You shouldn't be talking to the police directly about a client, unless there's a credible threat to someone's safety, but if you don't have that and you're certain that it's him . . .'

'What if I'm wrong?'

He clicks his tongue. 'The police ask a few questions then leave him alone, but if you're right—'

'He'll suspect I put them onto him. It'll get ugly quick.'

'Or he'll be extra careful not to put a foot out of line? And maybe the police find something that ties him to the fire.'

'Why don't I call Simms and tell him about Raze first? If Raze is the same person as my client, it won't matter.'

He thinks for a moment. 'That might be a better plan,' he says, before rising from the bed. 'I'm going to go finish washing up.'

•

You wouldn't describe sergeant Andrew Simms as excitable, but he is particularly downbeat when I call him.

'Look, this is bordering on conspiracy theory, Mrs Scott, but as always I'll note this information and give it due consideration when investigating this case.'

Annoyance swells in my throat. 'Due consideration? Someone online basically admitted to lighting the fire.'

'This kind of thing happens all the time. Do you know what trolls are?'

'Of course I know what trolls are.'

'Well particularly sick trolls often target people who have gone through a recent crime, the worse the crime the sicker the trolls. Some of the commentary surrounding crimes is particularly horrible. I would tell your son to take some time away from this online community and perhaps consider changing his alias.'

'The point is, Sergeant, Evan's identity should always have been anonymous. Someone at the very least has gone to the trouble of tracking him down. Doxing they call it.'

'Again, this is difficult to prove and even more difficult to pros-ecute. Doxing tends to be releasing private information to the public, not just *knowing* it. Most of these people are kids, and all we can hope for is a slap on the wrist from youth justice. So unless there is a serious crime, or we can prove a connection, we can't go pursuing everyone online who makes mildly threatening remarks. Again, as a courtesy, I'll check in with the cyber team to see if we can pursue this Raze kid, but I'll warn you again, do not meddle in the investigation.'

Mildly threatening remarks. 'The entire exchange has been really aggressive and quite sick actually; this person hates Evan.'

He sighs. 'Look, I wouldn't commit too much to the idea that this gamer is the one that started the fire. Last time we spoke you were convinced it was one of your clients. Which is it?'

I've been holding off saying this, knowing it will likely only make him scoff but I have to put it out there. 'What if it's the same person? What if he has been doing all of this?' My voice grows quick and manic, and I realise how unconvincing this sounds. 'What if he started seeing me to get to Evan?'

A light chuckle. *He's laughing.* 'I'll tell you what I told you last time: I think you should take a step back from it all and let us handle the investigation. As a psychologist I'm sure you can understand why objectivity is important and you'll only work yourself and your family up.'

Objectivity. He might as well call me an irrational woman. I can't rebut his point, though.

'I'll try not to put my nose in it any more.'

'If you would like any updates or have any questions, get in touch, but next time you have a hunch maybe keep it to yourself.'

'Sure,' I say. 'Sorry.' It's hard not to analyse people when I'm frustrated with them. Now I'm thinking of Simms as someone who grew up a loner, most of his interactions formal, stiff. He found a place he fitted in in the police force where uniformity and obedience are rewarded. He's a little like me in that he knows he must follow protocols and conventions, but unlike me, he's probably never broken them.

At night, I find myself listening to the peeling sound of car tyres on the rain-soaked pavement, the occasional sound of footsteps, the unfamiliar night sounds of this unfamiliar house. In the dark of night, I lie there waiting for the sound of shattering glass and the crackle of flames. I think about those words and wonder if maybe I really am being paranoid.

Next time u wont escape ;)

THIRTEEN

CORMAC ISN'T WORKING when I pick up my coffee but the girl is there, the barista. I stand by the coffee machine.

'Quiet in here today,' I say, looking around the cafe.

'It's not normally busy on Tuesdays.'

'Well, I need my fix and I love your coffee.'

She glances up. I can see freckles across her nose and although I can't see her mouth, her eyes tell me she's smiling. 'Thank you, I try my best.'

'You've worked here for while now,' I note, casually.

'Too long,' she says, as the milk steams. 'But it helps pay the bills while I slave away studying.'

'Oh, what is it you're studying?'

'Acting actually. I'm at Victorian College of Arts.'

'Great,' I say. 'You've got the looks for it. Not that that's the most important thing, of course.'

'Thanks,' she says, and her dark eyes tell me she is smiling again. She places the cup down on the counter, pushes a lid onto it and slides it forward.

'Extra strong latte.'

'Thank you,' I say, letting my gaze linger a beat too long on her face, before setting off. She still has a petite frame, despite her curves. She really is gorgeous.

I get to my office and wait for Xanthe. She's usually early but as the clock ticks towards ten, then past her appointment time I check the lobby again. 'Did Xanthe call in at all?' I ask Anna.

'No,' she says. 'She's due for ten.'

'Could you call and check how far off she is?'

'Sure,' she says.

I wait. I can hear the quiet murmur of the phone ringing, then Xanthe's voice and a beep.

'Voicemail,' Anna says. She moves the mouse, clicks, types. 'And we don't have a second number for her. I'll shoot her a text message and try her again if she's not here in five.'

I've got a bad feeling, a slow simmering in my stomach. In five she won't be here either. Something is wrong. I wait out in the lobby, reading over the notes in my pad, all those scribbles about Joe, the little observations I made. I read through his family history: working class family of four, father was a butcher, rough, but not abusive. Mother was a nurse, public school education, average intelligence.

I'm playing games less. I take drives at night. I've been having nightmares. I hear words like these every day from different clients, but they seem so much darker coming from Joe for some reason. I go to the back of my notebook and read through the information I had collected for my lecture later in the year.

We diagnose sociopathy by identifying certain criteria: a pervasive pattern of disregard for others, reckless disregard for safety of themselves or others, lack of remorse, indifference or rationalising the mistreatment of others. Diagnosis happens in a clinical setting because so few people with Antisocial Personality Disorder are self-aware enough to self-diagnose. There is a test formulated for that reason. High functioning sociopaths might be curious enough to take it, although they could just as easily reject the result.

I glance up. Still no sign of Xanthe. I continue reading.

Individuals with APD, that is the spectrum of disorders including sociopathy and psychopathy, tend to lack empathy and show signs of callous, cynical or contemptuous attitudes towards the feelings of others. It is a disorder much more common in males than females.

The door opens. I glance up, hopeful, but it's the delivery man. 'Good morning, ladies,' he says. 'Just a package today.'

'Thanks,' I say, signing for it.

I hand it over to Anna. 'Probably stationery,' she says as she tears the tape and opens the box. I'm walking back towards my office when she screams. 'What is it, Anna? What happened?"

She twists in her seat, finds the rubbish bin, and throws up. Rushing to her side, I find myself stroking her back. I don't want to know what is in the box, but I can imagine. I hold her hair back as she heaves. Then she sits up, her eyes watering. 'I'm sorry,' she says.

I turn, open the box. Blood, cartilage, bones. Dead people. Photos of dead people. But not just dead, maimed.

I close it again. Squeeze my eyes shut for a second but the images are burnt onto my retina. I feel nauseous. 'Shit,' I say. 'Don't apologise, Anna. This is sick.'

My limbs fill with cement. It's like the image left for me that night, only now they've sent them in the mail, so the box is trace-able, I think. So this might not be such a bad thing. There must be CCTV at a post office. I take the box out of sight into my office and dial Simms.

'I just got a package, a box with images, disgusting horrible images.'

'Slow down, what do you mean?'

'I mean someone has sent a package to my office and inside are—' I pause searching for an adequate description '—just filth, the most traumatic, disturbing images I can imagine.'

'A box full of them?' he says. 'Right, someone will be with you shortly. Don't touch it anymore. Maybe close up your office if you can until we get there.'

When the call ends I find my mind going to Xanthe. I tell myself maybe she just slept in. I go back to reception.

'Take the day off, Anna. Paid, of course.' I can feel a tremble in my arms and legs, my chest, like a scream wanting to get out, but I know I've got to keep calm, I've got to support her. 'If you need any counselling, or anything else I can help you with, please don't hesitate to ask.'

'I'll be okay, I can stay,' she says, her mouth downturned with the echo of disgust. She can still see the images in her mind.

'No, I want you to have the day off. Go rest up at home or visit friends.'

'Thank you,' she says, taking her coat from the back of her chair and pulling one arm into a sleeve. When she's ready to go, she grabs her keys and starts towards the door.

'They're fake, Anna,' I lie.

'What?'

'The images. They're not real. Gore scenes from old horror movies. They look real but they're not.'

'I thought so,' she says. 'But I just don't know why anyone would send them.'

'I know what you mean,' I say. She's a grad student. Soon she will be sitting in a seat like mine talking to people for eight hours a day.

'I'll see you tomorrow,' she says, stepping out onto the footpath.

I lock the door and call Xanthe myself, trying one last time. It rings out and her recorded voice comes down the line. 'This is Xanthe's phone, leave me a message.'

'Xanthe, it's Margot. You had an appointment booked in with me today at 10 am which obviously you've missed now. Please give me a call once you hear this to reschedule and let me know that you are okay. Speak soon.'

I hang up the phone and sit, waiting in Anna's chair for the police to arrive. I realise then that the image on my doorstep was likely left there before the fire. Maybe someone left it as a warning before burning the place down. Is this box a warning of something to come, too?

PART TWO

INTROSPECTION

Reporter: A man has died after a three-hour stand-off at an apartment block in Elwood overnight. Police arrived in response to a neighbour hearing banging from the apartment and the building was evacuated. The man refused to speak with negotiators and barricaded himself in his bathroom, insisting he would only speak with his psychologist. The man was known to neighbours as someone who had mental health issues. Police are not treating the cause of death as suspicious and no others were hurt.

FOURTEEN

IT'S BEEN THREE days. Other than Simms, the only person I've told about the box is Sarah, the dietitian. I'd knocked on the door to her room between clients, and sat down with her to explain what was in the package and why we needed to take extra precautions from now on. The police came and took the package away as evidence, but I assume if they had any leads from it, I would have heard. Simms told me they would dust for prints and attempt to trace it back to the original sender. Until they have the person who sent it, we have three new rules at the practice.

One, I open all packages, no one else.

Two, we never leave each other alone in the office. Which means coffee runs are a team effort if there are only two people here.

Three, we keep the door locked at all times. Patients press a buzzer and Anna lets them in.

The last two came as suggestions from Simms. He said they're just precautions, but his advice legitimised our collective fears.

I ran the Tan this morning but I found myself frightened, always looking over my shoulder for Joe. The fear is irrational, and I know it's pointless wasting energy on it, but some sicko is trying to mess with me. They're trying to terrorise me.

Between clients, I put light music on in my office and try to rid my body of stress. I meditate, I go through progressive relaxation techniques, tensing and loosening muscles until my body aches from the effort. I'm looking forward to my three o'clock session. At three o'clock I have Cormac. We were making progress last week, and I tell myself that's why I'm looking forward to it, but I know it's something else. Oddly, I feel like I miss him – only a little, but I do feel a bubble of excitement. I should call a colleague, another psychologist to discuss this with. But I know what they'll say: *countertransference, emotional attachment*. It's not enough of an issue to break off the professional arrangement, I need to just be mindful of it, to counter that bias I have towards him. I think about Joe and the advice I got to end his therapy. That's another decision I haven't made yet. It could provoke him, or it could be me needlessly losing a client, if this is all some bizarre coincidence.

As I come to the end of my session with Suzette, a bored, self-medicating housewife, I don't hear the buzzer at the door and consequently I begin to feel energy draining from me. Cormac hasn't arrived. When the session is up and I go out to the waiting room, I find he isn't there. But he was late last time. Maybe he's working again.

'Anna,' I say. 'Can you call my 3 pm and see how far away he is?'

'Sure.'

I stand there, listening. This happened with Xanthe, and now it's happening with Cormac. Something is very wrong.

Occasionally clients vanish without another word. Therapy does cost a significant amount of money and some people would rather disappear than admit that money is too tight for them to continue our sessions. Talking payment breaks the therapeutic alliance psychologists must maintain with clients, but that's not to say money should never come up. Money can but *payment* shouldn't; not until it's over.

I trust that Xanthe wouldn't leave without a trace, knowing I would be worried about her. Xanthe's absence was chalked up to coincidence by Simms when I spoke to him but how many coincidences does it take before they investigate? In a podcast I learnt about circumstantial evidence: each piece of circumstantial evidence is like a strand and when you have enough to form a strong cable there is sufficient strength to pursue the case in the legal system, even if one strand is weak, or a few strands break, just so long as the rest are strong enough. Have I reached sufficiency with Joe? Are there enough strands?

'Hi Cormac,' Anna says and I tingle with relief. 'I'm calling from South Yarra Pysch, how are you?' A pause, and I can hear him murmur down the line. 'Sure, I totally understand. So you won't be able to get in today?' she eyes me, her nose wrinkled. 'Okay, Cormac. Let me see if she is available to speak.'

She mutes the line. 'He wants to speak to you. He won't be able to make it in.'

'Why?'

'He said they won't pay for him anymore. Should I ask for a late cancellation fee?'

Shit. Adam must have stopped funding the sessions. 'Okay, no, that's fine,' I say. 'Tell him I'll call him back in a moment.'

'She'll call you in a minute.' She hangs up. I note his number on a Post-it and go into my office, where I make the call.

'Cormac, hi.'

'Margot, I'm really sorry to do this. I should have called earlier.'

'It's fine,' I say. 'What's happening?'

'Look, I can't be seeing you. He's not paying anymore. I think I'm going to try to sort myself out, get back on my feet and make a plan, maybe apply to another university. I wanted to pay for the visits myself, to keep seeing you, because I know it was really helping, but I just can't afford it.'

I can hear the sadness in his voice.

'I'm sorry, Cormac. I don't know what to say.'

'It's not your fault. I really wanted it to work, I know I'm reckless and self-sabotaging, I know. But I want to make myself better. It seems weird but I wanted to do it for you.'

I swallow hard. 'That's nice, Cormac. You've come a long way already. You've made progress.'

'It's not proper, I guess, but could I take you for a coffee some-time, as a thank you? No therapy, just a coffee.'

Say no, Margot. This is a clear boundary; psychologists must not socialise with clients. Another voice says, he's not *technically* a client anymore. That's hardly a viable defence if the medical practitioners board found out. But they won't – how could they?

'Just a coffee and a casual chat to say thanks, no pressure.'

I exhale. It feels like I would be letting him down if I don't. Finally I say, 'When were you thinking?'

'Well, I was looking forward to seeing you today, but it's prob-ably too late.'

'Today is fine. The day is almost over for me, so I can meet you after my next client.'

'Oh, really? That would be great.'

I can feel myself letting go. I can feel myself giving in to something.

'There's a place near me, The Pearl.'

'Sure, okay. I'll be there at five-thirty.'

'Perfect,' he says. I can hear the smile in his voice. I hold the phone next to my ear even after we've hung up, contemplating in the silence what I have agreed to.

My next appointment goes too slowly. Willow is a borderline, a little like Xanthe except a couple of years older. Willow has a habit of keeping me over the end of her appointment. She is needy, with attachment issues, issues with her parents and no real friends.

But today she's good. You're always looking for signs in your clients, reading their body language and mood. Willow sits up, straight-spined, one knee across the other. I keep one eye on the clock the entire time. I can't concentrate. I'm already there, meeting Cormac. When he said he wouldn't be coming back it felt like a break-up, the same emptiness, the same longing. He, like Xanthe, has the type of unique psychological landscape that drew me to this field.

But what is this meeting? A goodbye? After my final appointment, as I quickly pack up my office, replacing the empty box of tissues, I find myself reminded of my father. *Is Cormac like him? Is that why I feel like this?*

'Come on,' I say to Anna who is still at her computer checking the schedule for tomorrow.

'Oh, are you done?'

'Getting away early,' I say. Sensing my impatience, she quickly stands and pulls on her coat. I follow her out the door.

I lock up, then walk up the street to my car and fall into the driver's seat. I set the GPS for The Pearl.

It's too late to change my mind. That's what I think when I see that I am not meeting Cormac at a cafe, but a wine bar. *The Pearl:* I should have guessed from the name. Not many cafes are open this late. It's all black steel and big windows, almost hidden, signless apart from the opaque ring decal on the window. *You can still change your mind, Margot.* But I can't. *Just like the home visits to Peter.* No, that was different. That was a naïve young psychologist working as a case manager for the Melbourne Mental Health Service, a role that was more about checking in with patients who had left institutions then it was about administering psychological advice. Back then it was a rookie's mistake; this is . . . somehow different. This is an experienced clinical psychologist about to engage in a potential breach of conduct.

I peer through the front door, scan the faces of the people in the muted lighting. I don't see him. Good, not too late to make an escape. Maybe he won't show.

But when I turn, I see his familiar shape, striding towards me. He's so close, his gaze falls on me, and he smiles.

'Cormac,' I say, suddenly nervous. 'Hi.'

There's an awkward moment. Do we shake hands? Do we hug? In the end, he simply turns and opens the door for me. I choose a booth at the back corner, dark leather, and sandalwood. The type of place where men take their mistresses to drink cocktails. We sit and a waiter materialises.

'Still or sparkling?'

'Still,' I say.

'Still is fine,' Cormac adds.

The waiter comes back with a carafe of water, he fills the glasses already on the table and places two menus in front of us, then leaves again.

'Cormac, this isn't a cafe.'

'No,' he says, as if realising this for the first time. 'I guess not. I walk past this place a lot. I thought they did coffee.'

'They only do wine and cocktails by the looks of it.'

'Wine it is, then,' he says.

'Cormac, I can't be here. I can't be doing this. It was a bad idea to come.' I reach for my coat, but Cormac touches my wrist so gently it's almost painful. The voices are loud, filling the space, so I find myself leaning towards him to hear his words.

'Just one drink, it's not going to hurt. Remember I'm not a client anymore. It's just me trying to say thanks.'

My face grows warm where his eyes are fixed and there is a prickling at my hairline. I lower myself back into the seat, the coat slipping out of my hand across my lap. I dig my fingertips in at my hairline and massage my scalp for a second. If I'd gone straight home from the office, the first thing I would have done is pour myself a glass of wine anyway. And something else he said sticks: he's technically no longer a client.

'Alright. One drink,' I say.

I look up and realise we are close. I can feel his breath, soft on my ear. I shuffle back a little.

He smiles, and glances down. I follow his eyes to my wedding ring and realise I'm turning it on my finger. A nervous tick I've had for years. If it wasn't my wedding ring it was my engagement ring before that, but Cormac might read it as something else. I glance about the dark place, guiltily searching for any recognisable faces.

'You could have chosen somewhere quieter,' I say.

The waiter comes back, bends and speaks, 'Any questions about the wine list?'

'No. I'll take a glass of the Backward Point Pinot Noir,' I say.

'I'll have the same,' Cormac says.

'Good choice,' the waiter says, before collecting the menus and receding back to the bar.

'So,' I say. 'How did you find out the university won't continue paying for your treatment?'

'Adam Limbargo told me that he wishes me all the best but he can no longer continue to pay.'

In his correspondence with me, Adam had been supportive of Cormac, so why the change of heart? I sense there is something else at play here; Adam had a gambling addiction, and although it wasn't stated when I met him for coffee, I'm sure he'd lost a significant amount of money. Maybe he's in financial trouble and can't afford to cover Cormac's sessions? The waiter brings over our two glasses of wine. Cormac holds his glass out to me and I touch it with my own, then draw in a mouthful.

'I'm curious about this relationship, Cormac.'

'How so?'

'Were you doing anything for him? Helping him mark papers or something?'

'No, nothing like that. I don't know why he wanted to look after me. He took a shine to me, I guess.'

I remember Adam's earnest voice when he spoke about his wife. *She's at the end of her tether.* He was stressed, and in retrospect it always seemed odd that he would fork out money for someone else's therapy when he evidently wasn't prepared to pay for his own.

'I don't know what to say,' he continues. He slides a palm up his cheek, and it rasps on the stubble. 'He seems like a nice guy. Maybe he thought that if I ever did anything with my life, he would have that social currency. That's why people like him have charity auctions and charity galas, right?'

'So you see yourself as a charity case?'

'Well, I am, aren't I? What else would you be doing here tonight?'

'You're not charity, Cormac.'

'Why are you here, then?'

'I don't know,' I say, honestly. When I was younger I was much more reckless. I'd always find myself in situations like this, with that feeling that something was immoral, more worried about being caught than doing wrong, and yet I was doing it anyway.

'It doesn't matter now. He's pulled the plug.'

'So he called you?'

'I actually called him.'

'Wait – you said he told you he was no longer funding the sessions.'

'That's right,' he says, with a guilty smile. 'I think he stopped paying *because* I called him.'

'Oh, Cormac, what did you say?'

'I just wanted to know when they would take me back at the university. I'd been seeing you and trying hard and he wouldn't give me an answer. We got into a bit of an argument and I may have said some things about him that I didn't mean.'

'Did you think about me when you did this? Did you think about the work we've been doing?'

I almost miss it, but briefly there's a note of sadness, of regret in his eyes. Then it's gone. That charming veneer is back. He forces a smile to his lips. 'He just started calling me ungrateful, you know.'

'Cormac, this is what I was talking about. This streak you have of self-sabotaging. You called him for the same reason you wrote other students' papers: you don't think you deserve to be in his class, and you didn't think you deserved his money so you act out to hurt yourself. I think you called him to *start* that argument.'

He swirls the glass, raises it and breathes in the smell before taking a mouthful. 'I'm worthless – they know it, I know it; the only person in this world who thinks otherwise is you.'

'What about your sister? What about your girlfriend? What about everyone at the university who knows how brilliant you are?'

I take a sip of my wine as I wait for his answer. He heaves out a sigh. 'The girlfriend is gone. She still texts and bothers me, but it wasn't working out.'

'That's another thing you've just set about to destroy isn't it? Another relationship.' I stare deep into his eyes. 'Will that be awkward at work?'

He gives a small laugh. 'Awkward is right. That's why I quit.'

'Oh, Cormac.' I can't help but laugh at the futility of it all.

'And my sister, she's becoming more and more like Mum every day. She's acting crazy, always saying someone is outside the flat. She's the one who ought to be seeing you.'

'She thinks someone was outside of your place?'

'Yeah, I told you. She's obsessed with this bald man. I think he's homeless, but she swears he's been watching us.'

A bald man? Could it be Joe? What would he want with my other clients?

'So what about you, Margot? What's happening in your life?'

Back to the questions, always the questions from Cormac. That's what makes him a charmer, because people's favourite subject is themselves.

'Nothing is happening in my life, Cormac. The same old.'

'How's the family?'

'They're good.'

'Can I ask you a question?'

'You just did.'

'A personal question?'

I take a long sip of my wine. The glass is almost empty.

'Do you still love your husband?'

The question is a clean cut, and it sinks in close to the bone. I feel heat rushing to my cheeks.

'That is not any of your business, Cormac. But the answer is yes, of course I do.'

'I'm sorry,' he says, with a laugh. 'I didn't mean to make you defensive.'

I pause, my cheeks hot. I think more deeply about the question. *Yes, the way someone might love their brother. Yes, but partly because of how much he wants me. Yes, I love the fact I have someone like him.*

'It's entirely inappropriate, Cormac. You know that.'

'I just know there are different types of love and you've got kids and it's been a long time.'

'I said this isn't appropriate.'

'Sure. I just wish I had that. I wish I had a woman like you for seventeen years,' he says, before draining the last of his wine. 'Excuse me.' He steps away from the table, towards the bathrooms. I take a moment to check my phone, I text Gabe.

Stuck at the office, be home asap.

Sent. Cormac comes back a few moments later. Then, before I know it the waiter is there, with two more glasses of wine.

'Oh, no,' I say. 'I've got to go Cormac. I can't be here with you any longer.'

'Just another glass,' he says. 'It won't hurt. Text your husband and tell him you're having a drink with a friend.'

'I've already texted Gabe,' I say.

'Gabe?' *Shit,* I think. I gave him yet another personal detail.

'Yes, I texted my husband.'

'Then what's the problem?'

I take the glass by the stem and have another sip. I can feel it working on me, the blood slowing in my veins. I feel relaxed. I study his face, those green eyes. He runs his fingers back through his hair. I place the glass back down on the table. If Joe really *is* Raze, then he would only be out to get Evan, not any of my other clients. So *why* am I so worried about Xanthe?

'You know, Cormac. I've heard there's a stalker in South Yarra. He is bald, a little overweight and very tall. Maybe you should take extra care.'

He raises his eyebrows. 'Is that right? I'll be fine,' he says. Beneath the black button up shirts he always wears, I can see the shape of his shoulders, the ropey muscles of his arms pressing the cotton. But he's still smaller than Joe, and it's not him I'm worried about.

'And your sister? All I'm saying is you should both be careful.'

'That's sweet of you, Margot. To look out for us,' he says, his voice getting quieter, so I find myself leaning in to hear him. I glance down and find his index finger is sliding up my own. Then he's leaning closer still. Then he moves smoothly and swiftly so our lips are touching. A moment passes before my hand comes up and pushes him back. I jerk my face away. My heart slams.

'No,' I say. 'I'm leaving, Cormac. That was completely inappropriate. I'm married.' I quickly glance around the wine bar again, searching for any faces I might recognise but the room is too dark and no one seems to be looking our way.

'I'm sorry,' he says. 'I couldn't help it. I'm falling for you, Margot. I don't know what it is.'

'There's no excuses.'

'Sometimes,' he begins, 'I feel like I will never escape the shadow of my father. Sometimes I feel like my impulses are milder versions of his own.'

His father was cheating. That's at the core of the family breakdown. I had issues with my own dad, too, and I find myself overidentifying, excusing his behaviour.

'If he hadn't done what he did, I wouldn't be here in a wine bar sitting with you. I wouldn't be seeing you at all. Maybe I'd be a normal person who could keep relationships and live a happy life.'

'I'm sorry, but I can't help you, okay? I'm leaving.'

I lay two twenty-dollar notes on the table and stride towards the door. Then I slip into my car, turn the key and head off. In the rear-view mirror I see him standing on the sidewalk, half dissolved in streetlight.

FIFTEEN

I'M SPEEDING THROUGH the city, forcing the USB cable into my phone, playing 'Alive' by Pearl Jam. If I interrogate the way I'm drawn to these songs, this music from my late teens, I might conclude that it takes me back to the last time I was truly content, a time when my parents were still together and I could do and be whatever I wanted. Then university happened and I was locked on this path, hoping to impress my father with my grades, always telling him I was doing better than I was. Telling him I was topping my classes and impressing my tutors, when in reality I was middling, passing with Bs and Cs. Then I was thrust into the profession, cutting my teeth as a case manager. Soon after that Peter died.

I thump the wheel with my palm. It's happened again: I've gotten too familiar with a client. But this time it's different. Still, I berate myself; why did I meet him? Why did I go there?

I'm almost home when I notice the white Toyota. I see Joe, his huge lumbering figure in the driver's seat. He's right behind me. He's following. What if he saw me at the bar? What if he saw the kiss? I glance up again. He's closer still, speeding up. Then the car indicates and turns off. I breathe again. It's not Joe – it's no one.

I pull myself out of the car with my bag, climbing up towards the house. The moment I open the door, the regret of the past ninety minutes grows deeper, a yawning chasm in my gut. Gabe rushes towards me. If he found out it would kill him.

'Did something happen?' he says, peering at my face, eyes narrowed. 'It's after seven.' *Can he smell the wine?*

'I'm sorry,' I say, glancing towards the kids on the couch.

'Alright,' Gabe says. 'Let's eat dinner, shall we?'

I go to the sink and fill a glass of water. Standing there drinking it, I revisit that night, after Peter had hung up the phone. I arrived at his apartment and saw the police cordon, the flashing lights ahead. I drove towards them, but an officer raised his hand, indicating for me to slow down. I turned in hard against the curb, opened my door and climbed out.

Cones were lined up. I saw three police cars and an ambulance. Peter had been right, he'd either be going to jail or for a long stay supervised in a hospital. Neither place was ideal for someone like him. A bipolar man who was otherwise well adjusted, except when he had episodes.

Knots of people looked on from outside the police cordon. I didn't look up like them. I knew that if I looked up I might lose my nerve. I was walking a tightrope as it was; I'd gone off-script, I should have stuck to protocol, I should have called in all my visits and reported all of Peter's behaviour.

Peter was in the bathroom. He'd locked himself in there, that was what the officer who called me had said, but I couldn't help imagining him falling from the window down towards us, I couldn't help but picture him explode against the pavement. A stone formed at the base of my throat when I saw the cameras. A TV crew was there already. He told the police he would only speak with me. I knew I needed to be careful and play this exactly right or the night would end badly for us both.

'Hi,' I said, approaching the cordon. A fresh-faced officer held up his palms.

'You can't get through here.'

'My name is Margot Scott. The—' I paused, searching for the right word '—*suspect* called me a moment ago. I'm a psychologist. I'm his case manager.'

He scanned me from head to toe, his eyes pinched with scepticism. I knew what he was thinking. I got it a lot back then: *younger than I was expecting*. I was twenty-five, and hoping in the following few years to start my own practice. The cop turned away, searching over his shoulder for someone.

'Alright,' he said at last, raising the police tape. 'Follow me.'

I strolled a pace behind him. They had negotiators for this, but I knew Peter intimately, and I knew why he was locked in there. I knew that his threat of suicide was credible but he would never hurt anyone else. But it was unlikely the police would take my word for it; a man with a handgun is treated as armed and dangerous regardless of the circumstances.

The cops evacuated the building, after the report came in of banging and screaming from Peter's apartment. The occupants from all the other apartments stood on the street in coats and dressing gowns, arms folded, faces bored, impassive, some frustrated. They knew it would be about Peter; they'd probably seen his sleepless eyes reflected in the elevator or as he passed them in the foyer. Shy, unassuming, but clearly troubled. He'd gotten thin, colourless and gaunt. He reminded me so much of Edward Norton when we first met, but his good looks had faded.

'Hi,' I said, when the clutch of officers looked up. 'I'm a psychologist. I'm Peter's case manager. I spoke to him a moment ago.'

An older man with a neatly clipped moustache and grey eyes cleared his throat. 'Right, well, we've got guys in there now. He's barricaded himself in the bathroom. He has a weapon.'

'I know,' I said. 'Please give me five minutes with him. I need to get close to the door. I can help.'

He looked sceptical. I thought about confidentiality and realised this was one of those moments that qualified as *extenuating circumstances*.

'Peter broke up with his high-school girlfriend recently and moved into this apartment to live alone. He has bipolar disorder and a history of suicidal thoughts and ideations.' I found I was speaking quickly but I needed him to understand. 'He has no history of violence, nor has he shown any indication that he would hurt anyone else, but there is a very high likelihood that he will hurt himself. I'm asking you to let me through. I don't need to see him but just to be close enough to speak with him. He won't answer the phone anymore; this is the only chance.'

A knot appeared at his jaw, I could see a decision being made. Sparks of metal on metal behind his eyes as two opposing ideas clashed: he knew he couldn't just wait it out, but he also knew he couldn't risk me or anyone else getting hurt. 'He told the negotiator you're the only person he would speak to, but he's armed. So I'm not letting you too close. You can go up there with a vest on.'

'Right, that's fair enough,' I said.

A cop lead me into the building. We climbed the stairs and the vest was so heavy that by the time we reached the door of his apartment, I was short of breath. It was busted inwards; the lock bolt had passed through the wood like an exit wound.

I paused. 'Is he definitely alone?' I whispered.

The cop nodded.

'Alright.'

I stepped into his apartment, it was dark and clean. I saw the bathroom, a bar of light escaping from beneath the door. There were more cops, head to toe in armour, wearing helmets with

Perspex visors. Rifles in their hands at the ready. They were close, but just out of earshot.

'Peter?' I said. 'Peter, I'm here, it's just you and me.'

A murmur. I couldn't make out the words.

I was there, talking with him, but suddenly there was an explosion in the bathroom.

The air around me was hot and full of noise. A hand ripped me back, and I was pulled out of the room and thrown to the floor. I remember voices yelling, the sound of boots on wood. A crashing sound, wood splintering. The cops rushing in and aiming their guns.

I let out a scream, with my wet face in my hands and my entire body shaking. I tried to steady my breath.

Even now I can see Peter's face in my mind. I imagine the gun, the bullet.

SIXTEEN

THAT NIGHT IN bed, I open my work laptop and email Adam Limbargo.

Hi Adam,

I'm writing to let you know that due to my workload, I am regrettably unable to continue seeing Cormac Gibbons. I am happy to put you in touch with a colleague at another practice who I think will work well with Cormac and pass on any relevant notes in the event you decide to continue his treatment which I would strongly encourage.

Thanks,

Margot.

'What are you doing?'

Turning, I find Gabe standing at the door.

'An email for work.'

He comes over and sits down with his chin to his collarbone. He issues a sigh. The inevitable conversation is coming and I don't think I have the energy for it. I was planning on using tonight to catch up on work, to continue gathering my notes for my lecture.

'What's going on lately, Margot?'

'I'm just stressed,' I lie.

'You're drinking more, you've been home late, disappearing for hours at a time on the weekend. Your entire personality seems to have changed.' It's not just frustration in his voice, there's a barb of resentment in the pronouns: *you're* drinking, *you've* been home late. It's as though it hurts him to address me directly. 'Is there something you need to tell me?'

I'm not sure what he's suggesting but I know I need to give him something. 'I'm sorry, Gabe,' I say, closing the lid of my laptop. 'It's been a little hard with the fire and everything, and I've lost a couple of clients. There's a lot on my mind.'

'What happened tonight?'

'I had a glass and a half of wine, after work. I'll try to be more mindful in the future.'

'Who were you with?'

'Just myself,' I say. The lie tumbles out.

'Just like on the weekend?' He doesn't believe me.

'I know it looks bad, but you've got nothing to worry about. I'm not out there on a date or anything.'

'You can see why I'm concerned, Margot? You've never acted like this. You've never gone for a drink by yourself, especially when we're all here at home waiting for you.'

'I'm even more convinced my client was involved with the fire, and I'm worried he might be stalking other clients. Now I have him in the morning and there doesn't seem to be any progress on the case from Simms.'

'What can you do?'

'I don't know.'

'Can you cancel?'

'I could – I should in fact – but that's not going to solve anything.'

'Your clients who reported being followed, could it be paranoia, or a coincidence?'

'It's unlikely it's just a coincidence, but possible.'

He scratches at his jawline.

'The thing is, one client reported being followed and hasn't been back since or answered her phone.'

He drags his palm over his stubble. 'Is there a duty of care to check in with her family or friends? To make sure she hasn't hurt herself or been hurt by someone else?'

'I wouldn't know how to get onto the family. Look, I'm sorry,' I say. Then I'm crying and he's pulling me hard against his chest, his hand working the base of my skull.

'Shh,' he says. 'It's okay.' I sob, hopeless and weak, melting into him.

'Maybe you were right to get the police involved,' Gabe says. 'Maybe we should try my idea, an anonymous tip? If you're convinced, if you saw him driving behind you, then it's not really a risk at all. The cops just need to get his prints then they'll be able to nail him for the arson, right?'

'Maybe. But what if they can't take his prints or they can't prove it? What if he figures out it came from me?'

'How would he do that?'

'I don't know,' I say. 'Maybe you're right. Maybe we should make the call and hope for the best. But I'm just so scared.'

'I'm scared, too, but we've got to do something.'

Prosecutor: 'Now for the court, please read the title and the highlighted lines in the next document.'

Simms: 'Documentary evidence – Exhibit C: Personal diary extract'

'I know there is an age difference, but I also know it doesn't matter. We kissed. I felt alive for the first time in years. I felt like things were all in the right place. This illness I have, it sucks the joy and meaning out of everything, small things like rays of sun on my neck to the big things. I know I should be here for the people I'm supposed to care about and look after. I should be present and they should be enough but they're not. My girlfriend, or ex-girlfriend now, doesn't know why I'm pushing her away, she doesn't understand what is happening in my life, but I did it for Margot.

When our lips met, I knew it was worth it, I knew we were meant to be together even if she wasn't supposed to be seeing me like that, so she had broken protocol to spend time with me. She will lose everything if we just decided to start a relationship so I'm going to wait. It's all a waiting game now. I have something to live for. I have love in my life. I have her.'

SEVENTEEN

GABE READS THE words we had prepared in that plaintive voice of his. 'That's right, his name is Joe and he has been stalking people in the South Yarra area. I also believe he was involved with a fire on Gilson Terrace.' I stand there listening with the tip of my thumbnail between my front teeth. It's an anonymous service, and his phone number is set to private but still I think about the possibility of this call being traced to me somehow.

Afterwards in bed he holds me from behind, and I hold myself as if it takes both of us to keep everything together. Meeting Cormac at a bar, Joe potentially trying to kill me and my family, and now we've prompted the police to investigate him. My career is a house of cards waiting for a gentle breeze to tip it over.

•

In the morning, I stop off at Black Bean cafe, I order a coffee and stand waiting. The barista isn't as effervescent today. *Cormac,* I think.

'How are you?' she says to me, without a smile or eye contact.
'I'm okay, it's been a long week.'
'Tell me about it.'

She places the takeaway cup down for me, I grab it and turn to leave as she starts the next order but then I stop. 'Can I ask you a question?'

She looks up, her perfectly shaped eyebrows rising. 'Sure.'

'Does the Irish guy still work here?'

She gives a small huff, somewhere between defeat and amusement. 'No,' she says. 'He quit, actually.'

'Oh, that's a shame.'

She raises her eyes to me again. 'A shame?'

'He seemed nice.'

'You mustn't know him very well.'

I head to my office. I'm carrying my coffee and my bag, when Anna sees me from behind the desk. She buzzes the door and I lean against it to open it. Sarah is with a client.

'Hi,' I say.

'Hello,' she says, formal, stiff. Her eyes move from me to the corner of the room and I see the big shape of him sitting there.

'Joe,' I say, glancing at the clock above reception. It's only 9:40 am.

'Sorry, I'm early.' His expression remains neutral.

Very early, I think. I push a smile onto my face. 'No worries, won't be long.'

I go to my office and set it up, placing two glasses and a carafe of water on the coffee table. I'm about to have a potentially dangerous man in a closed room with me. My heart is thumping in my chest. I knew this was coming but I didn't think I would be so afraid when the moment arrived. He's smart enough to know he can't hurt me here, with a witness sitting at the front desk, but still the thought chills me.

I take a moment to set my phone up, propped on my table to record the room. The clock ticks toward 10 am. I step out to reception.

'Come on through, Joe.'

He's reading something on his phone. He pockets it, gets up and walks past me. There are three seats in my room, two opposite each other and one to the side. Where someone sits and how they sit tells you a great deal about their personality and mood. Some people fall into the seat, some gently perch on the edge, some grip the arm rests like a nervous flyer. Some sit close on the seat beside me, some, including almost all of the men I see, sit opposite me. That's always been Joe, but today he sits to the side, close enough that he could reach out with his huge hands and grip my throat.

He places one ankle on his knee and sits back deep in the chair, with his arms folded and his paunch poking out against his shirt. A defensive body position.

I lower into my own seat and find myself leaning away from him. Then I see it, a scratch on his neck, near his Adam's apple. The type of scratch a fingernail might make. I fixate on it for a moment. He sees me looking but doesn't say anything.

'So, how are you, Joe?'

His head jerks in my direction. He looks at me. 'I'm not so good today, actually.'

'Oh?'

Now he huffs, leans over his knees and scrubs his hair with his palms. I feel the energy in the room become electric, like the moments before a storm. 'I had police turn up at my house this morning.'

My fingers squeeze the pen, numbing the tips. I swallow the stone in my throat and try to keep a neutral expression. I need to keep up the façade. 'Really? What did they want?'

He heaves a sigh, his head turning, a smile eventually surfacing. 'Well someone called them on me – they must have. Can you believe that? Someone called the police and sent them to my house. First, I thought it must have been my internet browsing history or something weird like that but I know someone must have called them. They turned up this morning, knocked on the door and said they wanted to talk to me about a fire. The whole thing was very embarrassing actually, with my wife getting the kids ready for school, and my neighbours all seeing a police car parked in my driveway.'

Keep it together, Margot. 'Well that sounds awful. And what did you say?'

'I told them the truth.' A pause, that smile again. Then he laughs and the skin beneath his jaw wobbles. 'It was just insane. I was at home when this fire supposedly happened. With my family. My wife told them, too. I know they're probably just doing their jobs, but it was like they knew something.'

I need to keep the conversation away from the fire. 'So the police visit upset you?'

'I wasn't angry at the police, no. I was angry at the person that must have called them. I'd love to know who it was.'

I shuffle in my seat. I try a new tack. 'Why do *you* think someone called the police, Joe?'

'You tell me,' he says. I can see anger in his eyes, as they scan the carpet. The air is getting hot between us.

'Someone thinks you're involved, I assume.'

His eyes shoot up to mine. His jaw moves like he is chewing something. He doesn't answer, so I try to direct his attention away, keep him calm.

'Have you been drinking much?'

'The same as usual.'

'And how much is that?'

'A dram of whisky every other night, sometimes more.'

'Do you ever do anything you later regret when you've been drinking?'

'Don't we all?' Now he is watching my face with such intensity I have to pause. For a second I think about last night, the drink I had with Cormac. I reach for my water and my hand is trembling. He sees it. *Keep it together, Margot.* That's what makes me good at this, I tell myself, calmness, distance, control.

'What's wrong?' he says, a light, mildly teasing note in his voice. 'You seem a little *off.*'

'Nothing,' I say. Could he have dissociative identity disorder? Could he be one man during the day and another at night? Viewing the sort of material Joe sees every day could cause someone to dissociate, to partition off part of their psychological landscape to protect themselves from the trauma of the images. 'It's nothing,' I repeat. 'Let's continue with the drinking. When you have been drinking do you ever feel like hurting anyone?'

'Not really, just arguments with my wife.' Again that light breezy note in his voice, as though this is fun for him.

Push on, I think. 'Joe, why do you always gloss over your childhood when I ask?'

His eyebrows rise. 'I guess I had a normal childhood. There's nothing there.'

'And in your twenties?'

'Again, it was normal.'

I watch his face. That dumb neutral expression is back. The phone camera is still recording on my desk. If I can get anything close to a confession it should be enough. Then I have another idea. 'Well, I want you to do me a favour, Joe. Whenever you feel like drinking, can you take a moment to answer a few questions on a sheet? It's a good way to reflect.'

'Like homework?'

'Yeah, just like homework. We've talked a little about cognitive behavioural therapy before.'

I stand and go to my desk, hairs rising on my neck. I deliberately take the wrong set of sheets from a drawer and hand them to him.

'Oh,' I say, looking down as if only now realising my mistake. I'm so close, it feels like I'm reaching an arm into the Lions cage. 'This is the wrong one, sorry.' I pull it, but he holds it for a second, still looking down, then lets go.

I stride to my desk, find the right sheet in a stack of ten. I take them all to him, then sit down.

'So, fill that out each time you reach for a bottle of whisky. It asks you to write down why you feel like a drink, how you feel after, et cetera. It's a way of developing mindfulness around the act, so it isn't simply an impulse. Then we can review your behaviour.'

'Right,' he says. His gaze lingers on my desk. I wonder if he can see my phone there, propped on its side. Or perhaps he's thinking about the sheets, wondering why I took them back the moment he touched them. His tongue runs along the inside of his lip.

I touch my neck, frowning. 'What happened here, Joe?'

'What?'

'Your neck is scratched.'

'Shaving,' he says.

That is not a shaving scratch, I think. 'You did that shaving?'

'Well, no, it was my wife,' he says. 'I was drinking and she tried to grab the bottle out of my hands. I didn't touch her or anything. I just held her off and she accidentally scratched me.'

I sense he's lying. 'Really?'

He looks up. 'I think we're finished.'

'Sorry?' I say.

He points at the clock. 'That's fifty-five minutes.'

He's right. I turn back with a smile. 'That went quick.'

I follow him to the side exit. 'Same time in a fortnight?' I say.

'Sure thing. I'll behave myself until then,' he says, then gives a laugh as loud and sudden as a gun crack. Then Joe slips outside onto the street and is gone.

As soon as the door closes, I take the top and bottom sheets from the pile he had touched, I gently place them into a ziplock document bag.

'Cancel my eleven-thirty,' I say to Anna as I head towards the exit. 'Tell them I've an emergency and I can see them tonight or reschedule for another day.'

I'm in my car with the ziplock bag on the passenger's seat, speeding towards the police station, before I've even considered the consequences. It's a breach of protocol if I'm wrong. But if I'm right, Joe is going to prison. Either way, I'll never have to see him again.

EIGHTEEN

'MRS SCOTT,' SIMMS says, lines appearing on his forehead as he raises his dark eyebrows. He inhales. 'How can I help you?'

At first the officer at the front desk was reluctant to get him. She wanted to know precisely why I wanted to see Simms, and what exactly I intended to do with the sheets of paper in the plastic bag. I could have called, I suppose, but I needed to give him the evidence. Eventually she called Simms to the front desk from the depths of the office.

'This,' I say, holding it out to him.

He frowns, reaching between the glass barriers for the paper. I hold it away. 'Wait,' I say.

'What is this? You're conducting surveys?'

'No. It's got his prints on it. The arsonist.'

Simms turns his head, looking at the other officer at the front desk. Then he closes his eyes for a moment as if trying to clear a headache. 'The *alleged* arsonist. How would you get his fingerprints?'

'Look, can you just run them? That's all I want. If they match then I can confirm who it is.'

'I can't do anything until you do some explaining.'

'Explain right here?'

'Come on through to an interview room if you like.'

Interview room. I imagine a camera in the corner and microphones. 'Can we go outside instead?'

Again, that sideways glance at the other officer. 'Sure, there's a food court across the road.' He disappears for a moment, a buzzer sounds, and the door beside the front desk opens and Simms comes through.

He leads me outside into the sun.

'I've only got five minutes,' he says.

We cross the road into a shopping centre food court. Simms orders a cappuccino with two sugars. 'In a takeaway cup, please.' Then we sit at a table.

'Before you say anything. *Someone* called in an anonymous tip and we had a suspect,' he says, giving me a knowing look, making it clear he is talking about Joe. 'But he has an alibi.'

His wife. Of course she's going to say that, isn't she? She sleeps while he is awake all night. She probably thought he was in bed with her when he was out.

'So you're not pursuing him?'

'Not until I have something a little more concrete than a late-night anonymous phone call.'

I level my gaze on his face, push the bag with the paper across the table and speak directly at him. 'That's concrete. Just check, please.'

'I'll run the prints to clear him because frankly Mrs Scott I don't want you to lose your job over a suspicion.'

'Thank you. That's all I wanted.'

The girl at the counter calls Simms' name and sets the takeaway coffee down on the counter.

He stands and walks over to collect it. I follow him. He takes a sip, then turns back. 'I'll call you when we've cleared the prints. This is totally unorthodox, but I can see it's troubling you. I would also add that even if the prints match, as unlikely as that is, it only proves he touched the print-out, not necessarily that he threw the bottle.'

'But you would know it was him.'

'We would think it was him, yes. We'd bring him in and talk to him.' He reaches for the bag. 'It's not always easy to pull prints from paper, but I'll see what I can do. I'll be in touch.'

•

On the way back to the office my phone rings. It's an unknown number.

I answer.

'Margot,' the voice says. I recognise it immediately by the accent. 'I'm glad I caught you.'

'Cormac, how . . . how did you get this number?'

'I never would have called,' he says. 'It's an emergency.'

My skin prickles with irritation. 'I'm hanging up unless you tell me how you got my number?'

'You called me when I didn't turn up.'

I had called him, but normally my phone is set to private. 'I'm going to end this call now and you are going to delete my number.' I keep my voice even, trying to mask my annoyance.

'Look I just wanted to talk to someone. My sister has disappeared.'

'Sorry?'

'My sister, she's disappeared, and, well, I thought maybe she had run away or was doing her own thing somewhere, but the man in the alleyway is gone now too. He used to come and go but it's been days since I've seen either of them. Am I imagining this?' My mind wanders to the scratch on Joe's neck.

'Cormac, I can't counsel you. Go to the police, tell them what you know, give them the description of the man in the alleyway. I shouldn't tell you this, but we've had issues with another client at my clinic. I can't say anything else but he fits the description.'

'Right,' he says. 'Well, thanks for the heads up. I don't know what I will do if something has happened to her.' He pauses.

'Would you be up for meeting me for a chat. You left in such a rush the other night.'

'No, Cormac. I can't meet you.'

'But you had fun, I know you did.'

'Even if I wasn't married, even if you weren't too young, you're a client.'

'So? Is there some rule against it? Seeing an ex-client?'

I don't answer.

'There is, isn't there? That's all that's stopping you.'

'It's a breach of protocol, yes, but I am *married*, and you forced yourself—'

'Forced myself?'

'You kissed me, Cormac. Not the other way around. So that's why I am ending this call now,' I say, pulling into a park outside of my office. I think of Peter, how it ended, the weeks of uncertainty as the inquest went on.

'You don't mean it,' he says slowly, and there's sadness in his voice. 'You don't mean that, Margot.'

'Please leave me alone now,' I say, ending the call.

NINETEEN

THE REST OF the day is long and slow. I let Anna leave at five, knowing that I will be with my last client until six, then I'll leave myself. At no point will I be alone. I try to focus that last hour, but I'm plagued by thoughts about the fingerprints, what it means if they're a match and what it means if they're not. The verdict is coming. When the session ends, I take payment and see the client out. I should leave. I know I can't stay there alone but when I check my phone, I find I have one missed call from Simms. The anticipation makes my chest weak. I call him back.

'Margot,' he says. 'I've got news. I'd suggest you grab a seat.'

'Tell me, what is it?'

'I ran the prints.'

I draw a breath. 'And?' There's a long pause. Too long. I can hear my heart slamming in my chest. 'What is it, tell me?'

He clears his throat. 'We have a partial match of the left thumb.'

'What does that mean?'

'It means with a likelihood of about ninety-five percent, he's touched the sheet of paper that was left on your doorstep. It looks like he's our guy.'

I feel I could collapse as relief surges through me. I compose myself. I knew it, I just knew it, the bastard. 'So will you arrest him now?'

'Well, listen, we almost always *know* who has committed most crimes, but that's not how the courts work. You need to be able to prove it.'

'We can prove it with the fingerprints.'

An uncomfortable moment of silence. 'Well, that's not quite true. Like I said today, we can prove that he touched that piece of paper that had the image on it. The police prosecutors would call this evidence flimsy, especially given how I came upon this evidence, but it's enough to bring him in for questioning.'

'You'll do that now?'

'I'll organise a warrant tonight, but if we can't nail him on a significant charge a good lawyer could get him off, and then it becomes harder, so I want to time this right.'

'What does that mean for me? I just sit and wait?'

He clears his throat again, is this a nervous habit or a throat tickle? It's beginning to grate on me. 'It means bringing him in this early is a risk, because now he knows that we're investigating him, so he'll probably be on his best behaviour. Sometimes with these things we're better off trying to build a case *before* the arrest.'

'Build a case? You have a case. It's quite clear that he did it.'

'That's not a case, though; it's one piece of evidence linking him to an item at the scene. We will bring him in for questioning, we will drill him to find holes in his story, but we need something to link him to the fire, not just the image.'

'I can't see him again. I'm going to have to cancel his appointments.'

'Absolutely. Take extra safety precautions. Try not to be alone at night. Make sure someone always knows where you are.'

'Sure, I'll be careful,' I say, realising I'm alone in my office, I've broken my own rule and the street is darkening outside. I can see the light still on at the bakers across the road. Someone is running a broom over the floors.

'Now that we have narrowed our focus, it should only be a matter of time. It's hard to keep all the plates spinning when you begin lying to the police. He might have mentioned something to a colleague, or maybe his wife will stop covering for him, or another witness could come forward. He might try to dispose of evidence, et cetera. With the arrest warrant we will be able to search his possessions and we should find more evidence.'

'What about stalking the other patients?'

'They would have to independently make complaints themselves.'

'Hopefully someone will speak up,' I say.

'I'll keep you posted,' he says.

'Thanks.'

'Keep safe.' Then he is gone. That's when I look up and see the lights die across the street at the bakery. There's a shape at our door. I see him. My throat closes, my hand is already dialling triple zero. *Joe.* He's here.

I glance over my shoulder. I could run for the side exit. I turn back and see him. But . . . the man is too short. And the hair is too long. It's not a man at all. It's a girl. My heart still racing, I peer at the girl's face, shadowed by her hood. *Xanthe, is that you?* Then she is turning and rushing away. I move to the door, unlock it, and peer outside but the girl is gone.

TWENTY

THE PHONE TRILLS. I open my eyes, and the screen light leaps into the stillness and dark of the morning. I reach for it and see the time: 6:12 am. Who the hell is calling me this early? With a pang of guilt, I realise it's not early at all. Until all this started with Joe, I was up every morning and running by 5 am. It's a private number. A storm is brewing in my stomach. This, I know, isn't good. Sitting up I bring the phone to my ear.

'Hello,' I say.

'Mrs Scott, my name is Jennifer McVeigh. I'm calling from the Richmond police department.'

'Yes, hi.'

'I'm calling to let you know that unfortunately there has been an incident at your property in South Yarra.'

'My property?' I think about our house, gutted by fire. Does she mean the clinic?

'What is it?' Gabe says.

I roll over, sit up.

The woman continues speaking. 'Between 1 and 3 am your practice was targeted by an arson attack.'

I feel sick, the storm inside growing turbulent. 'Shit. Alright, I'll come down.'

'There's no rush to get to the property. Firefighters have the blaze under control.'

'No, I want to come. I want to see.'

'Sure,' she says.

Gabe has a hand on my shoulder, watching me. The call ends and I turn to him. 'It's happened again. Someone firebombed the clinic.' I'm crying now.

He sits up suddenly. 'You're joking?'

'I wish I was.'

'Jesus Christ.'

'I'm going down there. They're on top of it, but I want to go.'

'Give me a minute,' Gabe says, rolling over, feet hitting the carpet. 'Is it too early for coffee?'

·

It's a black shell. The front window has detonated inward. Flames have blackened the walls and the ceiling but the structure is intact. The fire service have cordoned off the street. Is this Joe's retribution for reporting him to the police? He's systematically ruining my life, scaring away clients, destroying my home, my practice.

'Shit,' I say, as Gabe drapes his arm across my shoulders and pulls me against him.

'It's all insured: loss of business income, building, contents, everything. It'll be okay.' He's already thinking like an accountant.

'I'm not worried about that,' I say. 'He's targeting *me*.' I feel his arm tighten but he doesn't speak. He can't deny it.

I expect to see Simms but he's not there, just a couple of uniforms, an ambulance, for what purpose I don't know, and two fire engines. Stepping from Gabe's grip, I walk up to the yellow tape blocking one half of the road.

'Excuse me,' I say, calling one of the cops over. He turns and regards me. 'This is my business. Can you tell me what you know?'

'You own this property?'

'Yes,' I say. 'What happened?'

He walks over to us. 'We're still figuring that out. It was deliberately set, though. It appears as though the interior was burgled before the fire began.'

Closer now, it doesn't look so bad – a coat of paint, replace the glass and furniture. Another insurance claim. I'll have to find an alternative space until it's all repaired, which probably won't be for a while, not until the monstrous bureaucratic cogs of insurance claims start moving. My mind runs through the inventory: all of the files, office supplies, furniture, petty cash – it's all replaceable except for the client notes.

'Is it bad inside?' I ask. Wind rushes up the street, tousling my hair and chilling me to my core.

'It was confined mostly to this front area,' he says, pointing. 'But that's probably a question for the firefighters.'

'Sure,' I say.

Gabe speaks up. 'Any idea who did it?'

'Not at this stage, although most of the shops on this street will have CCTV, so hopefully we will get a clear image of the perpetrator.'

Joe was following my patients, Xanthe is missing, Cormac's sister is missing . . . What if Joe is trying to find one of my other patients? The fire at the house was started in my home office. What if he had broken in there first, looking for something? What if he lit the fire to hide his tracks? The police and firefighters are going to lock me out of here, just like they locked us out of our home. I won't have a chance to really see what is missing. Suddenly I'm rushing towards the building. Towards the knot of firefighters at the entrance. A hand grabs my forearm but I snatch it off and rush through the front door.

'Stop,' a voice says. 'Don't go in there.'

But I'm already inside, ducking the yellow tape. The acrid chemical tang stings my nostrils and the roof is dripping water, steam rising from where the carpet had been. I can still feel the heat of the fire. I rush through the door into my office. The flames didn't get through from the front but the chairs have been flipped, the drawers pulled out. Boots thump behind me, but I know exactly where I am going. I get to the filing cabinet in the corner and wrench it open. My heart drops. There's nothing there. Someone has taken the files. I search my desk, opening drawers, and realise my pen is gone. The Mont Blanc from my father with the inscription. *Introspection is always retrospection.* The firefighter snatches me back so hard I think my arm will pop out of the socket. He grabs me by the waist and drives me out of the building. *What were you searching for, Joe?*

'What the hell are you thinking?' someone yells. Gabe is there, leaning over me.

My entire body feels numb. He's got all my clients notes now. What is he going to do with them?

TWENTY-ONE

'THIS IS STRICTLY confidential.' It's Simms on the phone. It's been two days of hell. Two sleepless nights. Forty-eight hours waiting for my world to end. We've done nothing but worry about when the next fire will start.

I'd just made a green salad for lunch and was about to eat it. Placing my fork down beside my bowl, I reply, 'Of course, my lips are sealed.'

'We've arrested Joe on both counts of arson.' The relief is a drug, surging in my veins, fatiguing me. I close my eyes, squeeze a fist to my mouth. Simms is still speaking. 'His shoe-prints match those found around your home on the night of the arson. Some property from the clinic was recovered in the boot of his car along with other items tying him to other crimes.'

My voice trembles when I speak. 'Can I ask what other items?'

'Again, this stays between us, but we found underwear and personal items believed to be belonging to a woman who has been missing for a week. There were also images of other women including yourself.'

I imagine Xanthe, and Cormac's sister and all the other potential victims. Victims of what? Stalking? What would have come next? What if he decided stalking wasn't enough?

'So what will happen now?'

'We hold him and continue to investigate and build a case.'

'Will he get out before a trial?'

'He can apply for bail but it's very unlikely it will be granted given the nature of his offending and the risk he poses.'

'But he hasn't confessed?'

'Proclaiming his innocence. The usual story. We've got a solid case, though. His wife has admitted that she didn't know where he was when the fire at your practice was set.'

I knew it, she was covering for him. 'Can I collect the items he stole?'

'Not yet, no. They'll be kept as evidence. You won't get them back for a while.'

'Well, can you tell me what you found of mine? My father's pen?'

'Again, between you and I, there were mostly just patient files by the looks of it. But we did find a pen which matches the description you left with us.'

'Oh, thank you so much, that's great news.'

'Thank me when he's in prison. If we recover more of your items, I'll let you know.'

It means so much to me that pen. Dad had it for years before he gave it to me. I was always his favourite subject growing up. I'd sit across from him and watch him scribble notes as he asked me questions.

PART THREE

RETROSPECTION

Reporter: Overnight a man was arrested at his home in St Kilda East in connection with two suspicious fires in the South Yarra area, police say. One fire was at a house in Gilson Terrace earlier this month. The other was at a commercial premises on Toorak Road on Friday evening. The suspect, who is in his forties, is also said to be known to one of the victims.

TWENTY-TWO

GABE AND I are at lunch at the Korean place near the townhouse we lived in before July and Evan were born, when he was still a junior accountant and I was still a case manager. The place has barely changed in eighteen years; the same old man works back in the kitchen and his wife, now with a face full of wrinkles, shuffles about, wiping down table tops grinning and doling out menus. I have the bibimbap, steaming with a gooey fried egg on top. I still haven't told Gabe about Cormac, and now that Cormac is no longer a client, I'm confident he won't find out. I don't think I will ever tell him. There's no need.

'So,' Gabe begins, 'how's the new clinic going?'

The only space I could find at short notice was a little further away from the city. I know I'm likely to lose clients but it's the best I could do for now until the other clinic is repaired.

'It's good. A nice Art Deco building. We've got a dentist and a physio in the same office so it's a bit busier. I don't like using the old furniture, though.' I'd pulled my furniture out of storage, the same desk and chair I had in my practice a decade ago. Green leather seats that groan when you shift your weight. An old glass coffee table. My phone chimes and instinctively I reach for it. An email. It's from Adam Limbargo. *Curious,* I think.

> Hello Margot,
>
> I'm sorry to hear about Cormac but I wasn't paying for him. I wasn't sure if you were still seeing him or not.
>
> Adam

'What is it?' he says.

I'm frowning hard at the phone. I look up, meet his eyes. 'Just a work email.'

He smiles. 'You know, that old furniture served you well for years. You could do worse.'

'They were old when we first got them,' I say, looking back at the email. I punch out a quick response.

> What do you mean, Adam? Who was paying, if you referred him on? The university? Also, you must have known I was still seeing him when he called you?

•

I send the message and try to block out that needling concern. Gabe is talking about Evan's gaming. We've eased up on the supervision and restrictions with both the kids. I have more time to do my research, now that I'm not so stressed and preoccupied.

'He's doing really well,' Gabe says, which is apparently an acceptable way of describing someone's proficiency at playing video games. *Doing well.* Raze disappeared online, which is completely unsurprising. I guess Joe doesn't have internet access in jail. The first thing July did with her restored freedom was go to Hudson's place to tell him all about it. Which reminds me.

'What time is Hudson coming tonight?'

'Seven,' he says. 'I'm cooking. Can you please be home early?'

'I can try. I've got a five-thirty,' I say. 'But I'll leave straight afterwards. No more late nights for me.'

July is eighteen in a month. It's hard to believe she'll be an adult and leaving school for good in a few weeks. If she gets into medicine she'll be studying hard for the best part of a decade, but it's what she wants. 'I'm still worried about her, Gabe. We can't have her go through what she went through last time, not this close to exams. I'm not going to have some boy derail her career aspirations.'

'It killed me, too, to see her heartbroken like that, but you've got to let her learn to navigate the world of boys. You came out of it alright.'

I reach out and take his hand in mine.

•

After lunch, Gabe drives me back to the office. On the way, I get him to stop off to pick up coffees. 'Wait here,' I say, as he pulls in. 'I'll be quick. Long black for you?'

'Perfect,' he says.

I climb from the car and stride across the road. The cafe is quiet. I guess Friday afternoons are hardly peak time for coffee consumption. The barista is there, leaning against the counter behind the machine. You don't need to see her hands to know she is looking down at a phone. There's no one waiting for coffee, so I walk straight up to her.

'Hi,' I say. 'A skinny latte and a long black please.'

'Sure,' she says. I pay with my card. Her eyes are winged black and I realise now she has a tiny nose piercing. Beans grind, and she tamps them down.

Feigning curiosity, I ask, 'Remember the Irish guy that worked here?'

'The one you asked about last time?' she says, leaning on the bench, waiting for the espresso shot to come through. Before I can answer she is talking again. 'You're curious about him, aren't you?'

I deliver my prepared backstory. 'Well, I was talking to him about my work when I was here a little while ago and he asked if I had any jobs.' It's a weak lie but I'm hoping she doesn't probe it.

'He's hardly strapped for cash,' she says, steaming the milk. 'I don't even know why he took *this* job.'

'I think he was struggling with the costs of university or something.'

She gives a sudden little huff of laughter. 'He's got a big apartment in the Sirius building,' she says, pressing a lid on a coffee cup. 'I think he'll survive.' She slides the cups across the counter. The Sirius building, a deluxe apartment high-rise near the city. That can't be right.

'Wait, if he has a nice place, why *was* he working here?' I say.

'No offence taken,' she says, with a wry smile.

'Oh, sorry I didn't mean—.'

'It's fine, I know what you mean. He was only here for a couple of weeks. Maybe he just wanted to experience having a job like the rest of us.'

'Well, thanks anyway.'

'No worries,' she says, picking her phone up again. I turn and start towards the door. Gabe will be waiting. 'Oh, one other thing.'

I look back. 'What's that?'

'He saw you when you came in that day, when you sat there for hours. He told me you were his psychologist. He told me you've got a crush on him and that's why he kissed me. He said he wanted to make you jealous.'

My cheeks become hot. I barely even manage to meet her gaze.

'But I don't know what the truth is, and which are the lies anymore.'

TWENTY-THREE

AFTER LUNCH I get back into my office for my 1 pm. The afternoon is a steady crawl towards the weekend. My final appointment for the week finishes at 6:30 pm and I'm the last one in the office. I think about Cormac again. He's got a nice apartment, according to the barista, and that email from Adam was disconcerting. I check to see if he has responded before I lock up.

> Margot,
>
> I'm sorry if he put you through anything, please don't blame me and please don't let him know I'm telling you this, but he insisted on seeing you. I couldn't say no, I hope you understand.
>
> Adam

A wave of dizziness washes over me. What the hell does he mean? I read and reread the email, but it doesn't make sense. Adam set this up; he sent Cormac to me. Is Cormac a stalker?

I call Anna.

'Hi, Margot.' A thudding bassline in the background tells me she's at a bar.

'Anna, I'm sorry to call you outside of your work hours but I'm still at the office and need your help with something small.'

'Sure, let me go outside.' The music drops away. 'What's up?'

'Is there any way I can check who has been paying for a client?'

'What do you mean?'

'I mean where can I find that on the accounting software? Where the payments have come from?'

'Have you got the iPad?'

'In my hands, actually.'

'I'll talk you through it.'

Anna helps me navigate to the recent payments section. Cormac's sessions were all paid in advance on the day. After some scrolling, I find the payments reconciled against his account. The bank statement shows the transfers came from a Westpac account with the name "N. Schultz". *Not* "A. Limbargo".

'Got what I was looking for,' I say. 'Thanks, Anna.'

I go back to my work emails and reread the original, looking for any meaning I might have missed.

> His name is Cormac Gibbons and to say he is remarkable is an understatement.
>
> I caught your guest lecture in July. I was at the back of the theatre and didn't have time to say hello but I did love your take on *Evil as a Necessary Ideal*.

There was also the day I bumped into Adam after he sent Cormac my way, but he slipped into a taxi before I could really ask him any questions, with something like guilt in his eyes.

> Please don't let him know I'm telling you this, but he insisted on seeing you.

I gently tug on the thread of logic and it snaps when I realise Cormac knew who I was and insisted on seeing me. *Nothing* here is accidental. My heart is slamming, the swish and throb of blood in my ears. I decide to go straight to the source. In my office I unlock my phone and call Cormac. It rings and rings, but finally he answers.

'Hello,' he says.

'Who *are* you?'

'Give me a second.' The line goes silent, then he comes back on. 'Hi, what's this about?'

'Who are you really, Cormac?'

'Me?' he says, with a laugh that sounds oddly nervous.

'I know that you weren't sent here from the university. You sought me out and someone called N. Schultz was paying for your sessions not Adam Limbargo. What else did you lie about?'

His voice changes. 'It only took you a couple of months.'

'A couple of months?'

'For you to figure it out. I expected better, to be honest.'

My throat clogs with questions. 'Why? Why are you doing this? Wasting my time.'

'I'm sorry, I just needed help. I didn't make it all up, it's just I can't help lying sometimes. I knew you were the best. I saw a lecture you gave about evil and thought maybe you could help me. But listen, it's really not a good time, I'm actually at the airport about to jump on a flight. I'll call you in a day or two to explain. For now, don't tell anyone about me, okay? I don't want anyone to get hurt.'

Shit. It's almost seven, I see now.

'Wait tell me—' The line goes dead.

I'm running late and Gabe is going to kill me. I rush out the door, locking it behind me and start towards home. Joe is in custody, so why does it feel like I'm about to step on a bear trap? My phone vibrates. It's a message from Cormac, but I don't open it until I am parked up in the driveway. Hot bile rushes up my throat.

The image is of us at the wine bar. It's taken from a distance and the room was dark but it's quite clear what's happening. My face is pressed to his, my hand is up, and it almost looks like I'm holding his jaw when in reality I was raising my hand to push him off. There are more photos: me leaning close to hear him, me smiling at him. Someone else was there, watching. What if Joe and Cormac were working together? What if this was all some game they were playing and now that Joe has been caught Cormac is upping the ante. I send a message back.

What the hell is going on Cormac? What do you want from me?

A moment later a message comes through.

Wrong person.

What does that mean? I just spoke to him. I push my phone into my bag and walk to the front door. I'm only five minutes late. *Seven o'clock at the latest,* Gabe had said. I open the door and step inside and for the second time in less than a minute, I have to resist the urge to throw up. I feel dizzy, confused. He's there. Right in front of me, sitting on my couch, with his arm around my daughter. *Cormac.*

TWENTY-FOUR

'MUM,' JULY SAYS, uncertain. My shoes are nailed to the floor-boards, my face burning. 'Don't act weird please.'

'I'm very sorry,' Cormac says, his voice different. 'I should introduce myself.' His accent is gone, replaced with something stuffy, upper-middle-class Australian. I think of the last thing he said to me, *For now, don't tell anyone about me. I don't want anyone to get hurt.* Gabe is there on the La-Z-Boy and Evan sits at the table. They're all smiling, all putting on a show for the guest, July's boyfriend. Cormac *is* Hudson. Why did I never see a photo of him, why didn't I insist on meeting him earlier? *He doesn't send selfies,* July had told me. Then, when I was out, he dropped her home, met Gabe. He is striding towards me, his stubble is gone, his hair is slicked back, his smiling eyes have something else in them now. They have a secret shared between us. *I don't want anyone to get hurt.* The message burns hot in my mind: it was a threat.

'Hi, Mrs Scott, I've been dying to meet you.' He holds out his hand, and I take it. I feel his grip tighten and I can barely keep from wincing. The silence in the room is loud in my ears, the white noise of rushing water.

'Mum!' It's July.

'Hi, Hudson.' I find my voice eventually. My rictus smile hurts. 'Nice to finally meet you, too.'

Then he is retreating back to the couch and I'm dropping my bag by the door. I cross the room, take Gabe's glass of wine and drain half of it in one mouthful. I notice July has a glass, too, and Cormac. I lean against the table thinking for a moment, running through all the conversations we had. It's almost impossible for someone to totally conceal their true nature from a psychologist, so there must have been clues. He was acting, and he has put in a lot of work for this, but why? Now he is here, he must have a plan.

'So Gabe was just talking about the night of the fire. July told me about it, but I didn't realise it was so bad,' Cormac says, again in that genteel, soft-edged accent. 'There truly are some horrible people in the world, aren't there? I'm just glad they caught the guy.'

'That's right,' I say.

'You must meet a diverse group through your work.' He's talking to me, but I can barely look him in the eye. Narcissistic Personality Disorder, I'm certain now, and I hate myself for missing the signs. I know I've got to play along because if I don't he could expose me. He has the photographs. He has enough evidence to ruin my career and possibly my marriage. Tonight will be about control for him. He believes he is smarter, better prepared and has all the power in this situation – he's probably right on all three counts – and if he lost control, he could do anything.

'That's right, Hudson. I meet some real psychopaths. The most frustrating clients are the liars, the compulsive liars that can't live with their own miserable existence so they try to ruin the lives of those around them. It's frustrating because when the truth comes out they just end up hurting themselves more than anyone else.'

A pause. 'Bit bleak, Margot,' Gabe says with a laugh.

'Interesting,' Cormac says. 'And Gabe, you're an accountant. How did you get into that line of work?'

'I just fell into it, I guess. Was always good at maths and studied business and accounting at university.'

Cormac is wearing a Ralph Lauren shirt, pressed chinos and R.M. Williams boots. Gabe's words from a week earlier ring in my head. *He's a bit preppy.* He also has money. He is wearing hundreds of dollars' worth of clothes. The deeper the deception, the more concerning it is, I think. Who would go to these lengths to disguise their true self?

'That's nice, and July wants to work in medicine. You guys are such a clever family.'

'Hold that thought,' Gabe says, going to the kitchen. When he comes out, he brings a tray of roast beef with him, then freights the rest of the food in trips back and forth from the kitchen: mashed potato, peas, roast carrots and sweet potatoes. Finally a gravy boat filled to the brim.

We gather around the table. I keep one eye on Cormac.

'This looks incredible,' he says.

'So, Hudson. What do your parents do?' Gabe asks.

'My dad is a lawyer—'

'A QC,' July interrupts.

'Yeah, that's right, and my mum was a teacher but now she's a stay-at-home mum.'

'You still live at home?' I ask.

'Mum, don't probe,' July says.

'It's fine,' Hudson says. 'Yeah, I live at home, although Mum and Dad have been away for six weeks, so it's just been me and my sister.'

'His family also has a house down in the country.'

Is there a flash of annoyance in Cormac's eyes? Was that something he wanted to keep from me. 'That's right,' he says.

I can't eat a thing, I feel too sick with worry. 'Why didn't you go along with them – your parents?'

'They're on a cruise for their thirtieth wedding anniversary, so they just went alone. I didn't want to crash their romantic getaway, plus I've got exams coming up.'

'Law, right?' I say.

'Yeah.'

I finish my wine and top it up again.

'What sort of law?'

'Well, I want to be a barrister but I'm a long way off that for now.'

I want to push him, to fact-check his story and back him into a corner. 'So you're at the University of Melbourne, Hudson?'

He takes a sip of wine. 'That's right.'

'Who is your favourite lecturer?'

'Good question. I'm thinking you must know some?'

'Margot knows everybody, Hudson,' Gabe adds, with a chuckle.

'Well, I love Professor Limbargo.' I have the urge to slam my fist down on the table. 'He's been such a big help to me.'

'Sure,' I say. 'I know Adam Limbargo. Why did you choose law?'

'Mum, he's not one of your clients.'

I could laugh. Cormac's eyes meet mine just for a moment, the ghost of a smile on his lips.

'It's fine. Your mum is entitled to grill me,' he says. 'What sort of mother wouldn't?' July shoots me a look. 'I was attracted to law because I believe in justice.'

'Justice, or the justice system?' I ask.

'Well, justice. The justice system gets it wrong from time to time, but nothing is perfect.'

The justice system gets it wrong. The words echo in my mind, bouncing around.

'Now, before we begin, would you guys mind if I say grace? It's a tradition in my home,' Cormac says. This more than anything else makes me grind my molars, makes me grip the underside of the table as if bracing to flip it. This small act, this deceit. 'My parents are Catholic.'

'That would be lovely,' Gabe says. Cormac reaches over and takes my hand and July's hand. I notice everyone, including Evan and Gabe, have their eyes closed and heads bowed. It's just me, then I turn to Cormac and see that he is smiling as he speaks his lines, his eyes on mine, daring me to say something. I could take my knife and bury it in his eye.

'. . . we give you thanks for this wonderful meal, expertly prepared by Mr Scott, and thanks for our health and happiness.' He takes a second, his tongue flicks out, runs over his lips. And he gives me the smallest wink. 'We ask that you bless the food and drink before us and continue to watch over us . . .' His smile grows, with each word he rocks his head left to right. Could I oust him now, just kick him out? I already know the answer. He wouldn't walk in here without a plan and the photos are his insurance policy. '. . . we are all grateful to be enjoying this meal. Thank you for this exceptional company, a *snapshot* of a happy and healthy family . . .' A *snapshot?* He's toying with me, threatening me in front of my family. '. . . and this wonderful patch of weather. We are also grateful for the recent justice served in relation to the fire and pray that you continue to hold those that would harm us accountable for you are our saviour and our judge. Amen.'

'Amen,' Gabe and July repeat. Evan and I remain silent.

'That was lovely, Hudson. You've got a way with words,' Gabe says.

'Thank you, that's just so kind of you to say. It's my parents – they always insisted I speak the Queen's English and have good manners.'

'Well, you've got two ticks from us,' Gabe says, the hopeless sycophant.

'How old are you, Hudson?' I ask.

'I've just turned twenty-one,' he says, and you could believe it, except I don't. He passes for early twenties with a clean shave and his hair neat, but I know he's twenty-six, or at least that's what's he put on his patient declaration at his first appointment. He also had to show ID, which means he's got a fake driver's licence or passport for his Cormac persona. 'I know that's a little older than July, but I think you would both agree, she is remarkably mature for her age and four years isn't so great a gap.' I catch the blush creeping up July's cheeks as she stares down into her food. 'My dad met my mum when he was nineteen and she was sixteen and they've been married for thirty-two years.'

Evan's head turns towards Cormac. 'You said they were overseas for their thirtieth wedding anniversary?'

'Oh, of course, I meant to say that they'd been together for thirty-two years but married thirty.'

Then Evan looks down at his food, a frown on his face. He's not fooled.

TWENTY-FIVE

AFTER DINNER, I STAND in the lounge window and follow Cormac with my eyes as he crosses the street. Lights flash on a car as he unlocks it. A white Toyota. I send a message.

What the hell are you playing at Cormac?

Wrong person, he sends back.

Don't play games. I know it's you.

I mean you got the wrong person.

The message is sent with a smiley face that makes me feel sick with anxiety.

You mean Joe?

Wrong person.

A chill washes over me and I bite my cheeks hard, still watching the tail-lights of his car.

Enough of this. What are you doing with July? Why are you doing this at all?

I'm sorry I can't answer that.

Was it you? The stalking, the fires?

Sorry, wrong person.

A glass slips from my hand and detonates on the kitchen tiles.

'Shit, careful Margot,' Gabe says, rushing into the room, annoyed rather than concerned. 'I'll do these dishes. Go sit down.'

'No, it's fine,' I say.

'What's gotten into you? You've been off all night.'

The images on Cormac's phone would be enough for me to lose my licence to practise. Would Gabe understand if I explained it all? One thing I must do is stop July from seeing him.

'Sorry, darling,' I say, forcing a smile. 'I was just stressed about being late and it put me in a mood.' I think about a line from the lecture Cormac sat in on. *Evil is as random as genetic coding, that is to say it's not random at all. We inherit behavioural traits the same way we inherit hair colour. The only difference is that certain traits come out a lot more when nurtured.* Nothing is as random as it seems.

'There's no need to beat yourself up about it. You were only five minutes late.'

'Maybe I will sit down,' I say, digging a thumb into my temple.

'Good idea,' he says, taking up a dish cloth.

I go to the lounge, dizzy and paranoid. July is sitting on the couch, her lips turned up at the corners. I know what this will do to her, how boys can ruin girls for years. I need to talk to her, begin deprogramming her the way I would a cult member. I stand in the doorway and watch as July pouts at the phone. She's sending him a selfie.

'July, honey, can I talk to you for a moment?'

The smile slips from her face but her cheeks are still flushed.

'What's up?' she says.

I sit down beside her on the couch. She is tucked into herself with her legs bent beneath her.

'I just want to know more about your relationship. I feel like I don't know much about how you met Hudson.'

She turns to me, daggers in her eyes. 'Mum, please don't analyse him or try to counsel our relationship.' *Our relationship.*

I swallow hard. I need to be careful. Cormac might already be subtly turning her against me. I know most of his story is a lie, but one thing is true: he is exceedingly intelligent.

'No, I'm in mum mode, not psychologist mode, July. Tell me about him.'

'Right now?' she asks. I reach for my glass of wine and take a sip.

'Yeah. How did you meet?'

'I don't want to talk about this with you.'

'Oh, come on, darling. Tell me. Was it online or at the library, or where?'

'If you must know we met online.'

Why did he choose you? Who is this about? I ask myself. Did he start seeing me because of July, or did he start seeing July to mess with me? There is a third possibility. Maybe this is all about gaming. Maybe he wants to go after Evan. He could have tracked us all down online. 'And how long ago was it that you met?'

'Three or four months. We didn't meet in real life until about two months ago.'

Four months. Which means he made contact with July online before me. 'Things are moving quickly, then?'

'Don't, Mum.'

'It's just an observation, July. No judgement.'

She looks back at her phone. Another message has come through. I squeeze the bridge of my nose.

'I guess things are moving quickly, but I like him.'

'Have you met his parents?'

'Weren't you listening? They're away.'

'Oh, of course.'

'What about his friends? Or his sister?'

'Mum, what is this about?'

'I'm just curious, July. You've had your heart broken before.'

She rolls her eyes. 'I met his sister, yes. But he's focusing on his studies so hasn't been hanging out with his friends much. I thought that would impress you.'

'That's nice, July,' I say, drinking the last of my wine. So she has met his sister, or someone Cormac claims is his sister, at least. 'I'm glad you're happy.'

Cormac was dating the barista at the same time, and she had seen his place. The words feel sticky in my mouth, they're hard to get out, but I have to ask. 'Have you guys . . . been intimate?'

'Mum!'

Gabe leans through the doorframe, looking in. 'What's going on?'

'She's asking if we've had sex.' Her cheeks are flushed with embarrassment. When Gabe meets my eye I simply shrug. I feel like I'm in a game of chess and I have absolutely no idea what my opponent is doing, I just know that a move is coming, and if I don't figure it out I will find myself in checkmate. He was clever enough to manipulate me, a married woman. July stands no chance. I remember that someone had taken the photos Cormac sent me, which means someone else was there. Could Joe be Cormac's dad or uncle or much older brother? What if this is all some sick game they're playing together? Or what if Cormac is playing his own game and Joe is just a pawn, too? The thought takes shape as a hard knot in my stomach. What evidence do I have? I look down at the message thread and realise all of his text messages say *wrong person*. And then there is the photo message he sent of him kissing me. There are the payments. *N. Schultz*. The name means nothing to me. I was hoping something would click into place, a connection would appear through the fog. I suppose I'd better call Simms soon and do some explaining.

'Margot, what's going on?'

I swallow, eyeing July who is looking at her phone again.

'I just want to talk to her about Hudson. Put your phone away for a moment please, July.'

'I knew you would do this,' she says. 'I knew you would hate him.'

'It's more complicated than you think.'

She looks down at her phone again, a smile playing at the corners of her mouth.

'What?' I say. 'What's funny? I told you to put it away.'

'Margot, calm down,' Gabe says. I realise I'm standing too close to her.

'He's texting her,' I say.

'That's fine,' Gabe says. 'Why is that a problem?'

The room heats a few degrees. I just need to buy a day or two to speak to Simms, to work things out. 'I don't want you to see him until after all of your exams.'

'My last exam is in two weeks.'

'Two weeks it is then.'

'That's not fair!'

'Margot!'

'We own that phone, your father and I. So if I say don't use it' – an invisible force pushes me closer – 'I mean don't use it.'

'What are you doing?' she asks.

'Margot, is this the right way to go about it?' Gabe says, and I could slap him. But I don't. Instead I fix my attention on July, who is clutching her phone in her lap.

'Hand it over,' I say, reaching for it.

'No,' she says, twisting away.

'Give it to me right now, July.'

'Leave me alone,' she says.

I grab her hands, prying her fingers away. 'Let it go.' I rip it free, stumbling back.

'Give it back!'

'Unlock it,' I say, low and mean. 'What's he texting you?'

'Margot,' Gabe says.

'Unlock it right now!' The rage is sudden. It's him, it's Cormac, he's done this.

'Mum, you're being a psycho.'

'Unlock this phone or you won't get it back at all.'

The wall shakes. Gabe's palm is hard against it, his eyes on me.

'Stop it!' he says. 'Stop it, both of you.' I see those brown eyes imploring me. 'Margot, you can't just go through her phone.'

'Yeah, Mum. Give it back.'

'July, she was trying to talk to you, she asked you to put it away and you didn't so you can apologise to your mother.'

'Me apologise?'

'Yes. Hurry up.'

She looks at me, her eyes glowing with fury. '*Sorry*, Mum,' she says. A verbal eye-roll.

'It's fine,' I say. 'But you're not getting your phone back.'

'Give it!'

'No, I'm holding on to it.'

She gets up from the couch and strides away. The door slams as she flies from the room and up the stairs. A moment later her bedroom door slams too, and the house falls silent.

Then it's Gabe and me. He's just staring at me, setting me alight with his gaze. 'Well, are you going to give it back?'

'I can't, Gabe. Her studies comes first.'

'*Her studies!*' He repeats it like a punchline. 'So this has nothing to do with Hudson?'

I chew my top lip. 'I just think he's too old for her. And he's not who you think he is, Gabe.'

'She's growing up too fast, you mean?'

No, that's not what I mean. He's a psychopath. I swallow the words in my throat. 'Yeah, something like that.'

July has an iPad, so she can still message and FaceTime him. But if I unplug the wireless router she won't be able to contact him at all. I do that now, tearing the plug from the wall and pocketing the cable. Gabe follows me.

'I think you can hold it for an hour, Margot, a night at most, then you've got to give it back. It's not fair, and she's learnt her lesson, I'm sure.'

Someone is coming down the stairs.

'Gabe, I think Hudson has Narcissistic Personality Disorder. I think he's dangerous.'

Gabe's mouth opens but he doesn't speak.

'It's a long story.'

Evan comes into the kitchen. 'What happened?' he says. 'I was in the middle of a game!'

'Just tether the internet off your phone,' I say in a way that prevents any follow-up questions.

'Right, okay, whatever,' Evan says, retreating from the kitchen.

I take the bottle of wine, splash a little more in my glass and drink it quickly.

'What are you talking about, Margot?'

'Hudson is one of my clients. Except he had an Irish accent. It's a long story, but he's been lying to me the entire time. I don't know what his plan is, but there's a chance he's involved with Joe.'

'Right,' he says, his dark eyebrows lowering. 'You're certain it's him?'

'Dead certain.'

I open my messages and quickly delete the photo from the wine bar, before passing my phone to Gabe. His eyes run down the screen.

'What am I looking at? This doesn't prove anything.'

'Look, he's playing a game. I just want to get into her phone to show it's the same phone number.'

A dubious look passes over his face, followed by a deep sadness in his eyes.

'Assuming this is not some kind of mix up, how do you explain that to her?'

'It's going to break her heart. He's used her as a pawn to get at me. We need to be tactful, but we need to deprogram her. I'll talk to her now, but she simply won't believe it if I tell her what I've told you.' By the look on his face, I'm not convinced he believes me, either.

I climb the steps slowly and tap on July's door. She doesn't answer. I push it open. 'July, honey?' I say. 'I'm sorry.'

'Go away, please.'

'I'm going to hold onto your phone just for tonight, okay. I'll give it back to you tomorrow.'

'Why do you hate him?'

'Look, we'll talk about it in the morning. And it's not that I *hate* him. There's more to it than that.'

'I know you're doing this to punish me. It was so obvious. You can't stand him.'

'You're right, I didn't give him much of a chance.'

The phone is still vibrating in my pocket, every few minutes. How many messages is he sending? 'One night,' I say. 'You can have it back tomorrow.'

I call Simms and he's not particularly excited to hear from me at eleven o'clock at night.

'Mrs Scott,' he says. 'To what do I owe the pleasure?'

'It wasn't just Joe,' I say. 'Someone else was involved.'

'*All* of the evidence suggests it was just one offender. Joe is tied to both fires.'

'No,' I say. 'I think another client was involved.'

He lets out the world's longest sigh. I can imagine him pinching the bridge of his nose. But I was right about Joe, so I know he'll give me a chance to explain. 'Who is it this time?'

'A man in his twenties. He's also been dating my daughter and targeting my family.'

'Name?'

'Well, Hudson, that's the name he gave my daughter, but Cormac is the name he gave me.'

'Look, I'm going to ask you to sleep on it. If you're worried, I'll get a car to drive by your place. It's not uncommon for victims of crime to be paranoid.'

'It's not paranoia. I was right about Joe.'

'You were, but the fact remains, both fires appear to have been set by one person. This other person may be guilty of something, but they're not guilty of lighting those fires.'

'He could have set one of them, or driven the car. He could be an accomplice.'

'The whole thing sounds like a strange situation. I can see why it would be distressing to realise a former client was in a relationship with your daughter. It's—' he pauses '—just gone eleven, so unless you've got a new crime to report, I'm going to ask you to sleep on it. I'll have a car drive by to check in.'

'Alright,' I say. 'Sorry for bothering you.' I hang up the phone but don't let go, squeezing it tightly in my hand.

Prosecutor: 'Now for the court, please read from this sheet.'
Simms: 'Sure. Documentary evidence – Exhibit D Personal diary extract'

'It happened last night. She came over. It wasn't scheduled, it wasn't my idea. She wanted to see me. We kissed again and this time we did more. I left the woman I once thought was the love of my life for her. I've moved on now. Margot is my future, I can see that. She can keep me calm, keep the demons at bay.'

TWENTY-SIX

IT'S LATE. GABE'S asleep in bed where I left him and I'm sitting on the toilet in our ensuite, the only light coming from my daughter's phone screen as I punch in another passcode. Wrong again. Nothing has worked. I couldn't sleep and I wasn't just going to lie there all night, curling my thoughts in on each other in a cycle of anxiety, a snake consuming its tail. How could I possibly sleep knowing what he is capable of? *He was inside our home.*

Locked out from trying any more passcodes in July's phone for a quarter of an hour, I reach for my own phone instead and continue my search for N. Schultz. I try variations with the last name in Google.

N. Schultz Melbourne
N. Schultz Cormac
Birth N. Schultz 1994
Birth N. Schultz 1995
1996
1997

He has an apartment in the city, he's clever, educated and he has money. I begin with the private schools in Melbourne. I search within five kilometres of the city. There are dozens. One by one, year by year, I search N. Schultz and each school name.

N. Schultz Melbourne Grammar 1996, 1997, 1998 . . . and so on.

It's been an hour in this darkened room, maybe more, and still no results, still no access to her phone.

I try something else. Compulsive liars tend to find lies that have parallels to the truth. Cormac's story about Ireland was likely lifted from the same story I read. But his parents' relationship, the disappearance of his mother, they're likely to be closer to reality. His parents split up in ugly circumstances and he sees this as the genesis of all of his problems? Something happened, something that shaped him for the rest of his life. I try a new tack.

Schultz death

A result comes up in the news from February this year, only nine months ago. *Jenny Schultz.* Where do I know that name from?

I click the article and read.

Jenny Schultz, youngest daughter of Casino owner Greg Schultz, found dead.

The Schultz family was struggling to come to terms with the sudden death of Jenny Schultz at her home in Beaconsfield Upper on Monday.

"We are broken, desolate, we just can't believe it," her brother Andrew said as he confirmed the news.

I pause for a moment, thinking. Adam Limbargo had a gambling problem, I know that much. It must all be related somehow. I read on . . .

The former high-school teacher was pronounced dead by paramedics when they were called to her Beaconsfield Upper home at 1:35 pm on Monday, after her son Nathan found her unconscious. Nathan, who had driven to visit his mother, is

176

yet to give a statement but it is understood that Jenny Schultz's drug addiction was not known by members of her family or close friends.

A spokesperson for Melbourne police said on Monday night: "At this stage, we are treating the situation as an unexplained sudden death. Officers are working to establish the circumstances. However, it is clear that drug use was a factor."

Jenny Schultz was often an outspoken critic of her father's empire, including his stake in a number of casinos. When Greg Schultz died in 2014, it is understood she sold her inherited stake to her brother Andrew Schultz who now is a majority stakeholder in the company.

Through the turbulent sea of thoughts, the name floats to the top like a cork. Nathan Schultz. *Nathan.* A memory comes back to me. I've heard that name before, years ago. *Nathan.* I search on Google but there is nothing other than the articles about his mother. No social media; none that I can find, anyway. No LinkedIn, no school history.

I think about the fires, first at my home office, then at the practice. Someone was looking for something and now I think I know what.

Nathan.

I go back to the bedroom creeping on the balls of my feet towards the door. I grip the handle, slowly turning it then pull the door a millimetre at a time.

'You can cut the silent act.' Gabe's voice makes me leap. I close my eyes and inhale.

'I won't be long. I just need to check something. My notes were burnt but I still have some at our storage facility.'

'You're going to the lot now? At—' he reaches for his phone and light leaps into the room '—almost 1 am?'

'I won't be long.'

'It can't wait until the morning?'

'It can't, Gabe. I'm sorry.'

'Well, I guess you've made your mind up.'

'I'm sorry,' I say, before slipping from the room and gently closing the door.

I rush out of the house. The light is on in Evan's room but I don't slow down to check out why. I just run out the door to the car.

TWENTY-SEVEN

THE STORAGE FACILITY is in an old brick building. It's further south, near where we used to live before the kids came along. I climb out of the car in the dark, my skin prickling. I move quickly and silently, fear rushing through my veins, filling my limbs. A security light comes on as I approach the front door. The key pass swipes through and the lock clicks. Turning back, I scan my eyes over the car park behind me before entering the building.

Our unit is on the second storey, so I take the wide service elevator up, listening to the gears grind. The elevator opens and I walk the familiar path along the corridors, past all those identical doors until I'm standing outside 2109.

The building is too quiet and every footstep along the steel walkway echoes. I look up in the corners for the cameras, those conspicuous black barrels recording everything that happens here, but still I feel the hairs prickle on my arms. I use the key to unlock the door and wince as it scrapes open filling the hallway with a grating sound. Reaching in, I find the light switch.

Nathan Schultz, I think. *Where are you?*

I go to the filing cabinet in the corner, moving our skis and Gabe's old cricket bag out of the way. I shift some boxes, making enough room to open the filing cabinet. These are the only patient notes I have left, and the oldest. I pull the first drawer out and find dusty folders all tabbed with year numbers. This drawer only goes back to 2012. I pull out the next one. This one goes back to 2007. Finally I reach for the bottom drawer and see files dating all the way back to the beginning of my career. I used to study these files when I still had that thirst for knowledge. I go to the early files, flicking through the patients in search of one name. Most are long forgotten; I wonder where they all are now. My handwriting was different back then – tighter, neater. Then I find the file.

Peter.

I remember talking about his family a lot. Before I really got to know him, he told me about his girlfriend. The way she and he both despised her wealthy family. He told me about the fights they had. He told me she didn't make him happy and that his sadness was a weed rooted deep inside of him and I could help him pull it out. I would need to cut him open and pick every trace of it out or it would always grow back. He wrote poetry and lay on the roof of his apartment block, staring at the bellies of the white clouds. It was lust for me, wanting what I couldn't have and taking it anyway.

I read my notes, recalling the one time I met him outside of his house, getting so drunk we could barely stand. Walking home when it was very late or very early. Waking up in his bed. Then I told him I couldn't see him anymore and he began to wilt.

It's painful reading through my words. I see the name and the cement that was churning in my stomach sets.

He believes he is only holding on for his three-year-old son, Nathan.

Nathan. It all clicks into place. I press my palm to my chest, steadying my breathing, my heart. My mouth hangs open. *Could it be true?* After all these years. Cormac is Nathan. Cormac is Peter's son. My thoughts are moving so quickly, in freefall now. He's lost both parents and he blames me. There was something else he said, in one of our sessions, that never quite sat right with me. He blamed the other woman. *I hated her, maybe I still hate her. Maybe she didn't realise he had a family but still, if it wasn't for her we might have been different. I might still have a family.* He blames me for losing his family. I shake my head, replaying his words.

This isn't some game, I now realise. This is all about revenge. I hear a noise outside. My heart squeezes. Is someone out there?

But then it's silent. It was just the wind. I have to get out of here now. Something moves on my hand. I scream. A cockroach. I whip my arm so hard my hand slams against Gabe's golf clubs with a crunch. My breath is short and my hand throbs and the sound echoes up the corridor.

I rush from the storage unit, without turning off the light or closing the door. I sprint back, taking the stairs two at a time. My hand aches and my breath burns but I don't stop until I'm in the car, turning the key.

Nathan probably inherited a fair portion of the Schultz fortune when his mum died. The fact they were never married means he simply kept his mum's last name. He has the means and the motive. But he doesn't know that I know who he is. That's my single advantage.

I think about him now. July isn't responding to his text messages and he will be growing angrier. I press the accelerator hard, racing towards home.

Prosecutor: 'And finally, Mr Simms if you would be so kind to read this final document.'

Simms: 'Documentary evidence – Exhibit A: Personal diary extract.'

'It's all over for me. Jenny doesn't want me near my own child anymore and when she gives birth again, I won't be able to go near the baby. She's got enough money to make sure I'm out of their lives. Sometimes I think of the life I could have had, what I gave up for Margot and what she refused to give up for me. I can't leave the apartment, I can't do anything. I just sit here, the sadness piling on, until I'm convinced the floor is cracking and I'm falling, swallowed by the earth. Some days it's like that and some days it's like I'm light, like I'm losing mass, as though I'm just fading, silently disappearing.'

Prosecutor: 'Thank you. And now if you could skip to the third paragraph where the text is highlighted.'

Simms:

'Margot told me she shouldn't be coming over to see me at all. She told me I would be getting a new case manager because she will lose her job, her career and the seven years she has spent studying and working if anyone finds out about us, which I realise now is much more important to her than me. So she's found someone else. She's giving up on me and settled for normality and I'm finally accepting it. I'm accepting that I'll never be happy. I'm accepting that life is not for me. I don't blame her or this new man but I just wish it was different.

Gabriel, that's his name. She'll live her happy suburban life and wake up one day to realise how banal and meaning-less her existence has become, and I'll be rotting bones by then.

I thought she was different. I thought she needed chaos like me, not some fidgety paper-pusher. He's younger too, more her own age. He doesn't have the baggage, the mania, the depression, the spells of pure unadulterated insanity, and he doesn't have a son. I can't blame Nathan: he's only three years old and yet I know the fact of his existence doesn't make this any easier.

I'm so close to the edge now, a gentle breeze and I know I'll fall. I told her I would do it tonight—'

Prosecutor: 'That's quite enough, thank you.'

TWENTY-EIGHT

WHEN I GET home, I rush towards the house. Cormac could be waiting in the bushes, or behind Gabe's car but I get inside and lock the door after me. Upstairs, I notice the light is still on in Evan's room. I check my phone. It's almost 2 am. He must have turned it on and fallen asleep.

I push his door open and peer into the room. He's not asleep, I realise. He's at his desk, on his computer, his face in his hands.

'Evan, honey, it's late. You should be in bed.' He turns to me. He's crying again. 'Oh, Evan, what's wrong? You don't still blame yourself for the fire?'

'Get out,' he says, all teeth and wide eyes.

'What's wrong?' I say, stepping closer.

'Why?' he says. 'Why did you do it?'

'Do what, Evan? Is this about July's phone?'

He turns back to the computer and clicks something on the screen. It fills up with an image. I freeze, my eyes growing wide.

It's a still of me and Cormac, or Nathan as I now know him to be, my mouth pressed to his. Except you can't see Cormac's face, only mine, because my hand is in the air, as if delicately reaching for his cheek, obscuring his face.

'That's not what it looks like,' I say, anger in my voice.

'What? Are you going to tell me it's photoshopped?'

'No. It's . . . it's different, Evan. Where did it come from?'

'It doesn't matter,' he spits. He is raising his voice now, too. The last thing I need is for the rest of the family to wake up. I don't know what would be worse, Gabe seeing this or July. Cormac is trying to do to me what he thinks I did to his family. He's trying to tear us apart.

'Was it Raze?' I say.

'So what if it was?'

'Evan, you—'

'Just don't!' he cuts me off, so loud I wince. 'Don't try to analyse it, Mum. He posted it all over the forums, so all of my friends have seen. I've been staring at it for hours. I know what's happening. I know what you did to Dad. Raze said it's been happening for weeks.'

'Do you know who that is in that image? Do you know who Raze is?'

'I don't want to know. I don't care. You're cheating on Dad.'

'No, I'm not,' I say. 'That is Hudson, that's July's boyfriend. I think *he* is Raze. He's trying to tear us apart.'

His expression is complex; there's so much anger, but it also looks like he is going to be sick. Evan didn't trust him at dinner, and he still doesn't trust him now. 'I told you it's complicated, Evan. You might not understand, maybe you never will, but he's been manipulating me. He's a con artist and he's trying to ruin our family.' He is shaking his head subtly but I press on. 'He was seeing me at the clinic. He was seeing me for weeks before I knew he was your sister's boyfriend.'

'Why didn't you say anything, if any of this is true? Why did you just sit there at dinner?'

'Because he might be dangerous, Evan. Because I was scared. I don't know, I wanted to talk to your father about it before telling you kids, especially your sister, and I knew if I didn't play along, he'd do something to hurt us.' I pause, reading his expression. 'That photo proves I breached protocol in meeting him outside of the clinic. He can ruin my career. He convinced you he was your friend online then turned your clan against you. *You* know what he's like.'

I almost miss it, the doubt that flashes across his face before the anger returns. 'You can't deny it, Mum. Stop making excuses. Look at that, you're all over him.'

I step closer and read the caption. *Your mum is a slut.*

Now it's my turn to be angry. Cormac has gone too far. There's another voice in the room and when I hear it, I draw a sharp breath and squeeze my hands into fists.

'What is it?'

Gabe is standing at the door. There's no use lying or trying to hide it. I turn and watch his eyes move to the monitor. A moment of recognition. The anger explodes inside of me, spreading like a mushroom cloud up from my stomach to my chest, my head, my arms. It freezes my jaw, I can barely squeeze out a word. 'No,' I say. 'No, Gabe, let me explain.'

Gabe simply turns away and walks up the hall back to our bedroom. He never liked to fight in front of the kids. But he saw the photo, and now there are three spot-fires burning in the house. I don't know which one to put out first. *Cormac did this,* I think. *This is his plan.*

I rest my hand on Evan's shoulder for a moment. 'Go to bed, son,' I say. 'We will have plenty of answers for you in the morning.'

Gabe is waiting for me. He's sitting on the edge of the bed, his face in his hands.

'Tell me everything now.'

'It's not what you think,' I say. 'That was Hudson in the photo.'

He looks up and this time I tell him the entire story. I begin at the beginning. The email from Adam. Cormac's sessions. Other patients reporting being stalked. I tell him what Cormac told me. As I explain, I realise the true depth of the deception. Cormac's backstory he probably found online, knowing my curiosity would take me there, knowing the news article had parallels to his own life. A father tragically taken, a drug addict mother. I tell Gabe about tonight, finding out who N. Schultz is, all but confirming my suspicion that Cormac is Peter's son Nathan. Realising that Cormac's attacks have not been random, but revenge.

'Revenge? How is it revenge, when you helped his father?'

'That's just it,' I say. 'Because of the inquest, he probably thinks I must have been at fault.' I pause, realising that lying hasn't helped me at all so far. 'I wasn't entirely honest with you about Peter.'

'You went to see him and forgot to report it to the clinic. Home visits were supposed to be recorded. Right? That's why you got in trouble, a breach of protocol.'

'That's why there was an inquest, but in reality there was more to it than that.'

'What else, Margot?'

I chew my top lip, arranging the words in my mind before I speak. 'He . . . well, he fell in love with me.'

'He fell in love with you? How does that happen if you're just a case manager? You'd have to remove yourself, if you knew a patient had developed feelings for you, right?'

'I should have removed myself earlier, I know. A relationship formed. It was brief, but intense. Then I called it off.'

'A relationship? Wait . . . between you and a client. *And* he committed suicide?'

I wince. I've been over this so many times in my head. He was bipolar. He had carved another woman's name on his arm. I made a mistake, but it wasn't my fault. It was never my fault;

Peter was born with it, an imbalance in neurotransmitters. Some people can't be saved. 'Yeah, I mean it was soon after I broke it off that we met. I requested that another case manager take over. The trouble is, they found out from one of Peter's neighbours that I had visited at night and it had not been recorded and reported back to the crisis centre.'

'And you didn't think to tell me at the time?'

'I did, remember? I told you I had come out of a rocky relationship.'

'I didn't realise it was with one of your patients,' he says. Then he does that shrug sigh. He's still hurting: all the lying, the years of keeping a secret and now kissing Cormac.

My phone is buzzing. A bit late for a message, I think, but it keeps buzzing. Cormac is calling me.

'It's him,' I say to Gabe.

Before I can stop him, Gabe has grabbed the phone and has it to his ear.

'Listen here, you little *shit*. Leave my family alone.'

I can hear Cormac's calm voice. 'Gabe,' he begins, 'I'm going to give you two very clear directives. One, do not call the police. If you call the police I will kill your daughter. Two, hand this phone to your wife . . . now.'

Kill your daughter. But she's here. Then it dawns on me, and I set off down the hall. 'July!' I rush towards her room. 'July, honey?' My voice is desperate. I throw the door open, and the cold air blasts me. It's cold because the window is open. I hit the light. Her bed is empty. I run to the window and look down into the night. The fire escape – she's climbed down it.

I turn. Gabe is in the room now. His expression is grim, in his hand he holds the phone, thrust out in my direction.

'He wants you,' he says.

I take it.

'Where is she?'

'The fun starts now, Margot.'

I scrunch my eyes shut and press the receiver to my face. 'Don't you dare hurt her.'

'It's not about her. It's about you.'

'I know who you are. Peter, he was your dad.'

'Is this the part where you talk me out of it? Is this where you tell me it's not my fault? This isn't *Good Will Hunting* and this story doesn't have a happy ending for you, Margot. Maybe for your family, if you're lucky, but not for you and me. Like I said, I believe in justice.'

'He was a manic depressive,' I tell him. 'He had made two suicide attempts before he turned the gun on himself. Your own mother would have told—'

'MY MOTHER IS DEAD!' he roars.

'I know, I know. I'm sorry. Just tell me where July is. Let us have her back and we won't call the police. We'll pretend it never happened. She has nothing to do with this.'

Then another call is coming in, a FaceTime call.

It's from Cormac's number. I accept. But I don't see his face. I see something else. It's July, with tape over her mouth, tears flooding her eyes. There's a gun to her head.

Then the camera turns back to Cormac.

He's smiling. 'I make the rules. This is what's going to happen. You, Margot, are going to get in your car and drive to meet me. If you call the police, if I even suspect you've called the police, I will kill your daughter. If you end this call, I will kill her. It's simple. Do exactly as I say and I will let your daughter go. Don't do as I say and I will kill her.'

'What are you going to do to me?'

His grin grows. 'I'm going to free you of your guilt.'

'What does that mean?'

'Go to your car, Margot, time is running out.'

'But what if my battery—'

'There's a charger in your car. Go now. Time is of the essence.'

'You can't go, Margot,' Gabe says.

'I can hear you, Gabe,' Cormac yells. 'Listen to this.'

A gun shot. I scream. Gabe reaches for the phone but I snatch it away.

'That's a warning. This thing is loaded. If any of you call the police, I'll kill her. Now go, Margot.'

I realise Evan is at the door, watching us, tears running down his cheeks.

'You heard what he said,' I say to Gabe.

'That's right, Gabe, you heard what I said,' Cormac smirks.

I have no choice. I can't let him win. I can't let him hurt my daughter. As I walk towards the door, I see Evan is holding something out to me at hip height. I take it. It's his phone. I don't say another word to them as I march outside, slipping Evan's phone in my pocket.

'Come on, chop chop,' Cormac says.

'Where am I going?' I say.

'Not so far. Just follow my directions.'

TWENTY-NINE

'SHARE YOUR LOCATION with me,' he says, when I'm in the car. I do. 'No wrong turns, no doing anything other than exactly what I say.'

'Where do you want me to go?'

'Head towards the motorway.'

'Will you let her go, after?' *After what?* I can't dwell on this thought for long, I can't let fear get the better of me.

'That depends.'

'On what, Nathan?'

'Don't call me that.' It's a hiss, a warning. 'My name is Cormac.' He hates his name. It represents something – his family? His mother? His past? *Cormac* represents his fantasy of coming from poverty, an origin story worthy of him. It wasn't just for my benefit. He was living the delusion to escape the reality. Multiple personalities perhaps? Trauma does strange things to the human brain. There are few things as traumatic as losing both parents suddenly and independently.

'I know about your mother's family.'

He sniffs.

'I know that you have all the money in the world but no real family to speak of.'

'Not true,' he says. 'You don't know about my family. I have a girlfriend, too.' I note the language he uses. *Girlfriend.* Not captive, but girlfriend.

I try to drive calmly, indicating at a set of lights, navigating my way through the streets. I steady my breath, and think for a moment. I decide to take a risk. As I round a bend, I let my hand slip off the wheel and knock the phone from the cradle. It hits the floor of the car, landing face down.

'Shit, sorry,' I say. 'I'll just pull over.'

I reach for Evan's phone and turn it to silent, as I wheel the car off the road. I remember something else Evan told me. *I've disabled all location services on my phone.* So they won't be able to track my movements.

'Hurry up,' his voice is muffled.

'Sorry, I'm just pulling over.'

I call Gabe's number and see that he has answered. I put the phone back in my pocket.

'*Hurry up!*' he screams.

'I'm sorry,' I say, reaching for the phone. I pick it up, place it in the cradle.

'If that happens again, it's all over. Understand?'

'Yes,' I say, starting out again. 'I'm sorry. Can you just tell me where I'm going?'

'No,' he says. 'Follow my instructions.'

'Sure,' I sigh. 'How did you get to Adam Limbargo?'

'Adam liked to gamble.'

Maybe he was in more trouble than he made out last time we met. 'You paid his debts?'

'I paid his dealer enough to keep him away.' *His dealer.* Adam was itchy, a little excitable. Addicts tend to have more than one addiction. Years ago at university he was never absent from parties, always the last to leave.

'And Joe?'

'He was such an easy target when I found out where he worked. He was oblivious to it all, had no idea he was set up until the handcuffs were already on. You still believe he's involved? Oh, that's classic.'

I can't breathe. He's so calculating. 'So Joe didn't take the photos, then?' He wants me to acknowledge his genius, his cunning. So much of this is about ego; that's why he hasn't simply killed me. It's a sort of Rube Goldberg machine: he's watching all the pieces move, falling into place. He's admiring his work.

'Take the outbound entrance,' he says, as I approach the motorway.

A message comes through on Evan's phone. It vibrates in my pocket. *How can I check it without him seeing the phone.* I swap hands on the steering wheel so my forearm is blocking the camera's view of my other hand. Then I bring my left hand back to the wheel as though I'm using it to steer, but now I'm gripping the phone. I open the message.

Just do what he says until we can find you and July.

'So who took the photos at the bar?' I ask.

'Look at the screen,' he says. I glance away from the road for a second. I realise now that he's not with July. He's aiming his camera at another screen which is streaming from somewhere else. 'Show her who took the photos, sis?'

I see July, a gun to her head, then someone else leans down looks into the camera. My pulse beats at my temples. I feel dizzy for a moment. *Xanthe.*

'You,' I say, but I can't get any more words out.

She was troubled but not dangerous. There was something she said, something that didn't quite fit. When she was talking about her controlling boyfriend, she said she loved him. When I probed her about it she said: *You have to love your family, though.*

Cormac swings the camera back to himself now. 'She's a very good gamer as well,' he says.

Xanthe is a good gamer. *Xanthe is Raze.* A horn screams. I glance up, find I've veered into another lane in front of a truck. I swing back, just in time. The driver is still leaning on the horn. The interior of the car is suddenly hot.

'Careful on the road,' he says with a laugh.

'Xanthe,' I say. 'Listen to me, you don't have to do this.'

'She can't hear you,' Cormac says. 'And even if she could, she wouldn't listen. She's just as prepared to kill her as I am, so don't think she won't. She did such a good job setting the fires, particularly the one at your home.'

'No,' I say. 'No, you're lying. It wasn't her.'

'It runs in the family,' he says. He was always talking about his sister too. Everything sharpens into focus now. Xanthe *is* his sister. 'She wasn't quite so good at acting as me, so we decided that when she was in your office she acted extra unreliable. We wanted to show you a pathological liar, a borderline. That made it easier. She recorded all your sessions for me to listen to later, with all her slips of the tongue. When she acknowledged that *Jacob* was her family, Jacob being me, I realised we had to cut her appointments off. I made poor, unstable Xanthe disappear. She had good ideas, though: wearing the same boots as Joe when she set the fires. *Genius.*' He laughs now. 'You should have seen her stomping around in those things.' He pauses. 'You're coming up to an intersection. Turn right towards Mt Dandenong at the lights.'

'Towards Mt Dandenong?' I say, as loud as I dare, so that Gabe or whoever is on the other end of Evan's phone will hear.

'Did I misspeak?'

'No,' I say, turning right. 'So what about Joe?'

'It was Xanthe's idea. Did he ever tell you about the time he found a phone on the train?'

'Yes,' I say, failing to see where he might be going with this.

'Xanthe was sitting next to him. She got up but *oops* she left her phone there. He picked it up and took the phone with him to work, then he took it home, stopping off at the bottle shop for a bottle of Chivas Regal. Without having to follow him, we found out what trains he takes, where he works and lives. We bought him another bottle of Chivas Regal to say thanks for finding Xanthe's phone and he was so happy he invited us in for a cup of tea.'

I swallow hard, try to focus on driving, staying in my lane.

'Then it was simply a matter of finding a piece of paper to print the image on, and finding a couple of empty bottles in his trash to start the fires. We stole the spare key for his car, put everything in his boot. It was really quite easy, and you were convinced, weren't you,' he says, letting out a laugh.

'Genius,' I say, because that's exactly what he wants to hear. 'You pulled it off. You sent an innocent man to jail.'

'No, *you* sent an innocent man to jail,' he says. 'Now, eyes on the road, take the next exit.'

•

I barely speak for the next half an hour, I just follow his directions, occasionally wiping my sweaty palms on my jeans and trying to keep from crying. Evan's phone feels warm in my pocket; the call is still going.

Finally, I speak again. 'Your father, he had some very serious issues. Some people will never live a joyful and normal life,' I say. 'Even if he was alive, you wouldn't have the happy family you think, Cormac.'

'Shut up!' he roars.

I fall silent once more. The only sound in the car is the quiet hum of the engine.

'At the end of the road there is a gate. The padlock is open. Remove it and drive through.'

I stop, climb out and walk in front of the headlights. The air is crisp and my skin prickles. I open the gate, get back in the car and start down the gravel track.

'Now drive up beside the house.'

I roll along gently. The headlights cut through the darkness, finally settling on an old weatherboard house. It looks as though it has been abandoned for half a century, the slate roof thick with lichen, trees and bushes crowding round it. Next to it is a paddock, and I see a flat, dark pond.

Then I see him. He steps out, stark in the headlights, and approaches the car. He opens the passenger door and the call ends.

'Margot,' he says. 'So glad to see you. Hand me your phone.'

I hold it out to him. He takes it, stands up straight and pitches it out into the pond, then turns back to me.

'Get out,' he says.

'Where are we going?'

'Somewhere even quieter.'

'I want to speak to her,' I say.

He turns his phone screen to me and I see July. She's in a different position now. The camera has zoomed out. Her wrists and ankles are taped. She begins jerking and kicking when she sees me. Then the gun is pressed against her head and she becomes still.

'July,' I sob. 'I'm coming for you.'

Cormac turns the screen away.

'I said get out.'

I climb out of the car. He still doesn't know about the other phone, Evan's phone, in my pocket. Could the police be listening at the other end of the call?

'Come on,' he says, pointing. He leads me to his car. 'Get in the passenger seat.' He has a laptop set up on the back seat and another black device. It crackles. He pulls a hood down over my head, and instinctively I reach for it, feeling claustrophobic, breathless.

'Relax,' he says. I bring my hands down slowly.

'We're not travelling far.'

I can't see anything, but I hear the driver's door open and close. He turns the car around, the gravel crackles beneath the wheels.

Through a bray of static someone speaks.

'40127A is at the Kilsyth property, 8994 Shepherds Road. False alarm code 3144. Building is clear.'

'Copy that, 40127A. False alarm code 3144.'

It's a scanner. He's listening to the fire service. Another sound, more voices. This time it's the police. A traffic collision on the Princess Highway.

'What is that?' I ask.

'Oh, I had to keep you honest, Margot. I had to make sure you didn't call the police.'

Breathing is hard through the hessian sack. Fibres make my throat itch.

'But we don't have to listen to that.'

The radio comes on. Michael Bublé starts crooning. 'Oh, I love this track,' he says. I hear him drumming on the steering wheel with his fingertips.

I stay silent, hoping the phone call is still connected in my pocket, praying it doesn't make a sound.

'Not a fan, Margot?'

'No,' I say, trying to keep the panic from my voice. Through the music there is more noise coming over the scanner. Most of it is in code, voices speaking quickly, reporting from crime scenes back to a dispatcher. I can't follow any of it.

'Where are you taking me?'

'Now why would you want to know that?'

'Are you taking me to July?'

'No.'

'Where is she?'

'Oh, don't worry, she's somewhere safe.'

'We must be near Mt Dandenong?' I say.

'Good guess.'

I'm pushed deep into my seat as he takes a corner at speed. Finally he slows down, turns sharply into another road. Then the car comes to a stop.

'What's happening? What's that sound?' I say, trying to give whoever might be listening some clues as to where we are. 'Gravel?'

'Observant,' he says. His door opens. I hear footsteps, then the passenger door opens and he rips the hood from my head. I see the shape of another house in the darkness. I climb out and he follows me up to the front door. It's open, and he gestures with a sweep of his arm for me to enter. The house is dark, but my eyes quickly adjust.

'Big house.'

He doesn't answer. 'Up the stairs,' he says. I reach out with my hands, find the rail and climb with him just behind me. 'Now, go in the room at the end of the hall.'

I do as he asks. Again he is close behind me, his breathing heavier now. He's excited about something. I can feel the danger, feel the train tracks of pain rattling as it hurtles towards me.

'Can you turn the lights on?'

'Power is disconnected,' he says. *A clue,* I think.

In the room there are two chairs. Then I see what is above the chairs. A rope hanging down. At the end is a noose. A chill sweeps over the skin of my arms. Outside the windows I see only empty fields, steeped in the moonless dark of night, and off in the distance, the shape of a forest.

'Is that Mt Dandenong?'

'No,' he says. 'Yalingbo Reserve.' It slips out without thought. A hint. A clue as to where we are. I'm forming another question in my head, to search for more information, but then he speaks again. 'We used to come here to this house when I was a baby, when I still had a dad. I can't remember, of course, but I can easily imagine it. The three of us out here, me still a rug rat.' He pauses, and his voice changes. 'But that was before you, Margot. Before you came into his life. So now it's my turn to counsel you.'

The room smells of something, not entirely unpleasant, a chemical tang that is already giving me a headache. Cormac grips my wrists and pulls them back hard. The squeal of duct tape. I feel it binding my hands together.

'What are you going to do?'

He doesn't answer. Next he does my ankles, binding them tight.

I think about my daughter, the gun against her head, her wide terrified eyes. He lifts me effortlessly so I'm up on the chair.

'No,' I say, tears starting. 'No, please.'

He reaches up and pulls the noose down over my head, then jerks it so it tightens.

'Good,' he says.

I'm weeping now. Why did I come here, why did I listen to him? There must have been another way. July could have escaped, or maybe Xanthe wouldn't have had it in her to actually kill someone. My breath is loud and my body is aching with adrenaline.

'Now you're in place, let's begin.' He goes to the corner of the room and comes back with reams of paper. If I fall, I die. If the chair slips, I die. I must try not to move and focus on keeping my balance.

He sits down across from me, looking up at my face. 'Depending on how honest you are, Margot, that will determine what happens to you and your daughter. If you lie, I will kill you. If you lie twice,

I will kill you *and* your daughter. If you tell the truth, I'll let you both live.' A spear of ice passes through me. 'All clear?'

'Yes,' I say. 'And you will let me go home?'

He nods. He folds one leg over the other, leans forward and glances down at the sheets of paper in front of him. 'Forgive me, it's a little dark in here.' There is just one window in the room, directly behind me, with moonlight passing through. He aims the torch on his phone at the paper. It lights his face up from beneath, making it into a gaunt, frightening mask, his eyes shadowed like canyons. 'That's better. Question one. Did you fuck my dad?'

I sniff. 'Yes,' I say the word carefully as if it might dissolve in my mouth.

'Good girl. You're still alive. How many times?'

'I don't know exactly, four, maybe five.'

I can see his teeth in the dark. He's smiling.

'Did he ever warn you he was going to commit suicide?'

I heave a sigh. 'Clients often threaten suicide or express suicidal thoughts. Your father told me he was contemplating suicide a number of times and *every* time he did I recorded it and followed protocol by checking in with him.'

He clicks his tongue. 'You sound like a fucking politician, Margot. Do you realise how much you sound like a fucking politician right now? What's your final answer?'

'Yes,' I say. 'He did warn me he was going to commit suicide.'

'Did you worry he might tell someone that he was fucking his shrink?'

I try to shift my weight but the tape is too tight, and the wooden seat creaks beneath me. I know I can't lie. 'I did.'

'What did you do?'

'I asked my boss to assign another case manager.'

'The day before the night he committed suicide, did you visit him?'

'Yes.'

'Did he tell you that he was going to commit suicide then?'

I draw a long breath. 'Yes.'

'Did you follow protocol?'

I shake my head, then become still to keep my balance, suddenly feeling sick.

'I can't hear you, Margot.'

'No, I didn't,' I say, my voice growing louder. 'I didn't, okay?' Then I scream.

He steps forward and puts his foot on the edge of the chair, then nudges it so I'm clutching at it with my toes, only just hanging on. The rope is choking me as it gets even tighter. I can't scream now. I can barely breathe.

'One more outburst and I kick the chair away.'

'Please,' I say, gasping. 'I'm going to fall.' He nudges it back in place so I can stand straight again.

'There's no point screaming. The nearest house is almost two kilometres away. No one is going to hear you. Now, tell me what did you do?' There's hunger in his voice.

'Nothing. I left him there.'

'Did you want him to die? Did you think he might tell someone what you did and ruin your career? Were you worried Daddy would think less of you?'

'I don't know.'

'That's awfully close to a lie, Margot.'

'I didn't want him to die,' I begin. I need to tell him what he wants to hear to buy time. I think about the question. The past is emerging from the shadows in the corners of the room. It rises like dust motes in sunlight. I close my eyes and let it take me. I'm visiting Peter. He was so manic, so out of control.

I can hear his voice. *'We had fun. I just don't understand, I'll never understand. I love you, Margot. You love me.'*

'No, Peter. This has to stop. I'm . . . I'm seeing someone else now.'

'I've got a gun.' It was sudden, stated plainly and I knew he was telling the truth. I knew he would use it. 'I'm doing it tonight.'

I froze for a second, I didn't know what to say, what to do. Peter had become a big problem for me. He was unstable, demanding, dangerously impulsive.

'You know they're going to put me away. You know if I don't do it I will crack.' If he cracked he might hurt someone else. He might hurt me. He might tell the wrong person about our affair.

'You've got options, Peter. You may not see it now, but you can be happy with someone else. You know that, right?'

I open my eyes, Cormac is watching me with a twisted smile on his lips.

'I didn't really, Cormac,' I say. 'I didn't want him to die, but it was inevitable.'

'Did you ever think it would be convenient if he died?'

I know if I speak I'll start to cry. The hard fibres of the rope scratch my skin.

'Did you?' he roars.

I start to cry. 'A little,' I say through the tears. 'Just for a moment I gave up on him. I thought there was nothing I could do. I am so so sorry, Cormac. I should have fought harder for him.'

Then he laughs.

THIRTY

'I WANTED YOU to have changed. I wanted to believe you were a better person. You met my father, you got drunk with him, you made him break up with my mum. You did this.'

'I didn't,' I protest, but he carries on as if he hasn't heard me.

'You killed him and then you just thought you would do the same again. You let me break up with someone you thought was my girlfriend. You drank with me. You kissed me.'

'*You* kissed me,' I say, regretting it instantly. The force of my words causes me to sway on the chair for a heart-stopping moment.

He continues speaking. 'Do you see what I am saying? You haven't changed. You don't regret what you did to my dad, do you? How could you when you would just as soon do it again. I presented an unstable patient profile, vulnerable, self-sabotaging and you still got too close.'

'You don't understand.'

'Oh I do,' he says, suddenly. He walks behind me, pausing in the square of moonlight coming in through the window. An angry hiss of paper shuffling. '*Margot visited me again today. We're falling in love . . .*' He drops a page. '*We kissed. I felt alive for the first time in years. She told me she wants to be with me . . . We kissed again and*

205

this time we did more. I left Jenny for her . . .' Another page falls. *'I can't blame Nathan, he's only three years old, and yet I know the fact of his existence doesn't make this any easier.'* Oh, this next one is a real doozie. *'I'm doing it tonight. I told her I have the gun. I told her if I can't be with her I don't want to live.* Remember that, Margot? It gets better. *She told me that she's with Gabriel now. She told me she can't save me.'* He circles me, dropping the pages one by one.

'Where did you get them?' I say.

'They were in my mother's things. She knew all along and she protected you. She could have ruined your life but she forgave you. She was too weak to do the right thing. She didn't blame you, but I do.'

'What were you searching for?' I say. 'The times you broke into my house.'

'Your notes on him. Anything to help me understand,' he says. 'This is the story so far. A woman falls in love with a damaged man. They have two children. The damaged man falls in love with his psychologist. She screws him, then *encourages* him to commit suicide. The woman lives a lonely sad existence with all the money in the world until she develops a drug dependence. She spends half her fortune on prescription medication, then one day her son finds her lifeless body.' He opens the window now, then goes to the corner of the room. The smell grows stronger. Then I see it, the can. 'Do you know who I blame, Margot? Not my dad, not my mum. The reason I am so fucked up is because of you.'

'I cared for him,' I say. 'I did. And I can help you.'

'Oh, you can *help me.*' He claws the air with his index and middle finger, making quotation marks. 'Just like you helped him? You're a pretty shitty psychologist if you call that *help.*'

'Please Cormac, we had a deal. I told the truth, I answered your questions. Now let me go.'

'This is going to kill July, really. She'll never recover.'

'You said if I told the truth, you wouldn't kill me.'

'You may not have lied,' he says. 'But I did.'

Then he circles me, rushing quickly about the room, emptying the can. The space fills with the smell of kerosene.

'You've got a choice,' he says. 'You can jump and kill yourself, or you can burn to death. Up to you.' He trails the fuel to the door and I hear it spilling as he walks down the stairs.

My heart seems to be the only thing moving. It's punching my chest. Around me is stillness like a drawn breath. Then I hear it, the sound of a match striking and the hiss of a flame.

THIRTY-ONE

A DOOR SLAMMING. The car starting. I'm all alone. I scream but I know there is no one for miles. I'll be long dead in the charred remains of a house before anyone can reach me.

I scream again and this time, over the growing crackle of the flames in the stairway, I hear something. A tiny voice, screaming in my pocket. *The phone.* The call is still on the line. I twist, carefully but still the chair rocks beneath me. I can see the flames in the doorway now, climbing slowly up the stairs. It crackles and hisses, moving in a line that spreads like ink and all the shadows grow and lean as the flames dance. It's coming. I can't get my bound hands to my pocket but someone is there, someone is listening.

'If you can hear me, I'm in a house,' I say. 'A house somewhere within fifteen minutes of Olinda. I think we were driving south of there.' *It's hopeless.* 'We took the road south, then turned left . . .' *What road was it? Think, Margot?* He'd turned hard, pushing me back into the seat. 'We took two lefts from the last house.' *But they don't know where the last house was.* Unless they found my car? More screaming on the phone. The flames are at the door now, entering the room. The silent march of fire. He'd circled me in such a way that at first the fire stays at bay, a perfect ring. The floor will likely drop through before I'm burnt alive.

I start screaming, but it's hopeless. No one can save me now. The flames climb the walls. The sound of burning grows. And I can feel the sweat all over my body.

My only hope is someone in the rural quiet hearing the fire or my screaming. I shriek. My throat aches. The fire is crackling fiercely now. I try to tear my hands free but the tape is too tight. It won't give.

I stand steady. He wants me to jump. He sought the symmetry between Peter's destruction and my own, but I won't go out like him. My last defiant act is to stand steady and take what's coming. The flames are encroaching on the circle, licking out towards the stacks of paper beneath the chair. The smoke is burrowing into the fibres of my lungs. I can't stop coughing. The room is so hot now, I feel the sweat in my hair, my lower back, my calves. The flames are hissing, screaming. *No,* I think. That's not the sound of fire. Turning back to the window, through the smoke, I see something. Lights.

My heart catches and I could cry. Over the crackle I hear sirens.

'Help!' I scream. 'Up here.'

I hear something, banging downstairs, then the flames start . . . *withering.* White foam. A man. Cormac must be back, this must be some sick game he is playing, but . . . it's not Cormac. He is dressed head to toe in yellow.

'Help!' I say. 'I'm over here. His hands find me, hold me for a moment. Then he reaches up and at once the rope loosens about my neck.

'Stay still,' he yells. 'I've got you.'

I fall forward, folded over his shoulder and we're moving. The stairs crack and his foot falls through but he clutches the rail and continues on. More sirens sound now, swarming around us.

I cough and blink through the sting of the smoke. The hoses start blasting the room. I can hear them spraying the flames. We burst through the back door, shepherded by two others.

They lower me onto the ambulance stretcher. More wails, more sirens. They're all coming, coming for me.

THIRTY-TWO

THE CLOCK TICKS on the pale grey wall in the boardroom of the Richmond police station. It's 4 am, and every minute that passes by means the chance of July coming home alive drops. Gabe goes to the watercooler and fills three plastic cups, bringing them over and handing one to me and one to Evan.

They treated me in the back of the ambulance before they would let me go with Gabe back to the police station.

They were insisting I go to the hospital, for smoke inhalation, but I refused. When the flames came closer, I was only thinking about survival, but now I'm thinking about July. I can't let Cormac win. We've got to find her. We need to do something.

Gabe hadn't called the police. Instead he called Simms directly and explained the situation. Simms's team had triangulated the approximate area of the house based on the clues they overheard and the mobile phone towers my phone had pinged. Then they had emergency vehicles patrolling the area, until one noticed a white Toyota racing out of a dead-end street. Then, as they got closer, they noticed the smoke.

'They've still not managed to make contact with him,' Gabe says, with resignation in his voice. The door opens and Simms is there.

'Come on through to an interview room,' he says.

We follow him down the hall, passing other cops, coming and going, all moving so quickly as though their kinetic energy alone might conjure July.

'Alright,' Simms says, closing the door behind him. He sits down across from us at the table. 'Time is of the essence, so you're going to run me through what happened tonight, the car he was driving, where he lives, what time you noticed your daughter missing.'

I recount everything I remember from the night and he keeps me on point, cutting me off when my thoughts meander or I begin to speculate.

'Just the pure facts,' he says. Gabe holds my hand in both of his and there's another cop in the room with us, making notes on a yellow pad.

Finally, when he has extracted all the information from me he can, he says, 'Okay, we've got police searching for the car, the plates have been sent to every cop in the state and we will continue to attempt to make contact with both Nathan and Xanthe Schultz. But our main priority is to find your daughter. Now I need you to think, Margot. Think deeply about Xanthe and Nathan. Was there anything at all that might help us find where they've taken July?'

I think hard about all the conversations with Xanthe. Cormac was too clever, too meticulous to reveal anything *real* about himself, but Xanthe was different. Where did she live? Close by, in an apartment maybe? Xanthe was playing games as Raze so . . . Then it hits me. *Evan knew the area she was in.*

'Evan,' I say. 'You had the IP address for Raze.'

His eyes go wide.

'What does that mean?' Simms says.

'I can show you,' he says. 'I just need a computer with the internet to log on.'

Simms stands, opens the door and gestures for us to step outside. We march down the halls back into the crisis room. Simms hunches over the long wooden table and taps the password into a laptop. Then he steps back, pulls the chair out for Evan and says, 'All yours.'

Evan slides in, opens a browser and accesses his gaming account.

Simms calls over two other cops, and all of us gather around as Evan navigates his account. He had sent the IP address to another gamer, and when he pulls up the message he copies and pastes it into an IP look-up.

"Pakenham East" comes up and beneath it is a map with a large blue radius.

'So the IP address used was in this area,' he points.

'Can you narrow it down in any way?'

'Me?' Evan says. 'Well no, I just know that they're somewhere near Pakenham East based on the IP, but they could be running a proxy to hide.'

'Pakenham East,' Simms says, turning to one of the other officers. 'Check to see if either of the Schultzes owns property near Pakenham. In fact, let's get a list of any properties owned by either of them, beginning with anything in this radius,' he says, thrusting a finger at the screen. 'Then we can check in with all of them, working backwards.'

'The mum,' I say, now remembering something else. 'July said something at dinner, something that annoyed Cormac. She said he has a place in the country. He might have told her about it, knowing he was going to one day take her there. Maybe he was telling the truth. But it's not just that,' I say, turning away from the screen, locking eyes with them all one at a time. 'I read in an article about Nathan's mum that she died at her home. It was in the country somewhere—' I pause, thinking, trying to remember the suburb. Meanwhile Evan is tapping away at the keyboard. He pulls up the article, scrolls through it.

'—Beaconsfield. It was Beaconsfield Upper,' he says.

'That's it,' I say.

'Alright, let's start there,' Simms says.

'We can contact their ISP for personal information from the account,' says one of the cops. 'But it will take a while.'

Simms turns to us. 'We're pushing it out to the media, which means there will be photos of your daughter on the breakfast shows, they'll be talking about it on the radio and—' he checks his watch '—it's too late for print media but it will definitely be online the moment we send out the press release, which will be any second now. I just want to prepare you. We can also organise a media liaison. The best thing for you to do now is to go home, support each other.'

'No,' I say. 'I can still help.'

He doesn't say anything. He just looks at my face for a moment.

'We will stay out of the way.'

'Fine,' he says.

'I've got a J. Schultz in Beaconsfield Upper, 4291 Beaconsfield – Emerald Road,' one of the other cops says.

They've still not made contact with Cormac or Xanthe, but if she is at that house, I wonder how they would approach it? Even if they knew July was inside, there's no telling what Cormac might do when the police close in. As if reading my mind Simms says, 'Let's get a team ready to go. Nobody use the scanner. We'll have to make do without.'

It all seems so simple, but I know it won't be. My daughter is out there alone and terrified at gunpoint or she's already . . . already what? I can't begin down that path; it'll sap any energy I still have and leave me a shell. I have to believe she is okay, that she will survive this. I refuse to believe that something has already happened to her, something irreversible.

THIRTY-THREE

WE'RE IN A waiting area, sitting on sticky plastic chairs near the front desks. We watch people come and go to report missing wallets or other miscellaneous crimes and outside the pink glow of dawn begins to spread. Then it begins. There's energy in the building, raised voices. Police, I know, are at the house. Why have they not told us what's happened? Evan hunches forward with his face in his hands. Gabe lays his arm over my shoulder pulls me against him. I can't stop thinking about Cormac, his words are in my head, bouncing around my skull.

Finally a door opens and Simms comes through.

He draws a deep breath, and something grips my heart. 'There's news.'

'What is it?' Gabe says with urgency.

'We've got her,' Simms says. Something unlocks inside of me and relief rushes in, filling my body. I don't cry, or let out a gasp, I just sit, watching Simms's face.

'She's on her way to the hospital.'

The hospital. 'What did they do to her?'

'Nothing,' he says. 'She's fine, it's just a precaution.' He gives his head a small shake, like a hound snapping at a fly. 'Don't worry.

There was teargas used, and she's got minor lacerations from the binding around her wrists and ankles, so she'll be treated at the Epworth.'

'And she's safe,' I say. 'You're certain she's safe?'

'I'm certain,' he says, with a small nod. But I won't believe it until they have Cormac in custody. I won't believe it until I see July with my own eyes.

'And Nathan and Xanthe Schultz?'

'Xanthe is in custody but there's no sign of Nathan yet,' he says. 'He inherited a number of properties when his mother died, so we're checking each of them now, but he could be staying anywhere. He could be planning to travel interstate, or perhaps even leave the country. We can stop him at customs of course.'

'No you can't,' I say. Simms's brow falls in concern. He rolls his tongue around the inside of his top lip. 'He's too clever to use his own name. He had a fake ID when he turned up for his first appointment, so he's probably got a fake passport or a boat, or some other way of escaping.'

'It's not just people scanning through your passport stamps,' Simms says. 'They have facial recognition—'

'He'll find a way,' I say, and there's resignation in my tone. 'He's a narcissist, prone to over-confidence in his own abilities, but he's also extremely detail-oriented. Everything has gone to plan, except for the fact Evan gave me his phone. If not for that I would have burned to death and we might not have found July at all.'

'We will certainly be aiming to stop him, whatever he's planning,' Simms says. 'The media will be showing his image so he won't be able to get in a taxi, let alone board a plane, without someone recognising him.'

What if he has a private plane or his own driver? He has enough money to do anything, I think to myself.

'Well if you folks want to head out to the hospital, July will be there now.'

•

At the hospital, we close in over her. Even Evan hugs her. I find myself combing my fingers through her hair as she recounts the night, with tears streaming down her face. She's already been through it all with the police. Cormac wasn't there at the house. She didn't see him at all. The last message he got through to her iPad before I disconnected the router was a message telling her to meet him out on the road at midnight and so she climbed down to the street and rushed to his car. She was so angry at me at the time, she says.

'I'm sorry, Mum.' She starts crying again. 'I'm so sorry. I got to the car and his sister was there. She told me he had organised for her to pick me up. Then she drove me out into the country and that's when she pulled a gun.' The grief spills over. It'll be years of therapy to undo the trauma of this single night. July had very strong feelings for Cormac. 'She drove me to that house then kept me tied up in a chair. I thought I was going to die, I was certain she was going to shoot me. I was there for hours and she wouldn't talk to me, wouldn't say anything. She just stomped around the house. When the police came she was in the kitchen, looking out the window, watching the trees. Then the room exploded. The door smashed down and the room filled with smoke. My eyes were stinging. I heard her scream, then a thump as she hit the ground hard beside me, then they tackled me too and held me down.'

'Shh,' I say. 'It's okay. We can go through this later. Just rest now, July. It's all over.'

I stay like that with her, holding her together as best I can, and soon enough she is dozing off in bed. Gabe is there too, holding her hand. Evan is in his seat, his eyes shadowed with dark rings.

My own eyes are warm, with an itch beneath the lids, as I focus on my phone screen. It's 8:11 am. I open *The Age* newspaper app. The first story is about last night. I see an aerial photo of a house in the dark. It's wrapped in police tape, with blue uniformed officers milling about, taking photos and laying out evidence tags. The title reads: Girl Saved in Late Night Siege.

The article mainly talks about Xanthe but also mentions her accomplice for the kidnapping, Nathan Schultz. It warns that he is on the run. I can imagine their wealthy relatives, deeply involved in the casino, like the uncle, whose net worth is reportedly in the hundreds of millions, seeing the headlines and calling in favours to keep an arm's length from the kidnapping, the siege and the rest of it. Perhaps they're already sending cease and desist letters, organising lawyers for Xanthe and Cormac's defence. Or is it possible the black sheep of the family, the son and daughter of his ungrateful sister, will be cut adrift and left to fend for themselves?

I know Cormac will find a way to get a minimum sentence, even probation. They'll produce an adequate excuse, drugs and trauma, then the rehabilitation will start. His Ted Bundy-like charisma will knock years off the sentence. A sympathy piece on *60 Minutes*. Then they'll be out and they'll come after me again.

I step out into the hall with my phone and call Simms.

'Any news?' I say.

'Not yet, but we've checked every property they own, and nothing's turned up. His primary address was listed as an apartment in the city but it's empty.'

'The Sirius building, right?'

'Sorry?'

The barista's voice rings in my head. *He's got a big apartment in the Sirius building.* 'He lives there.'

'Umm, no,' he says the word slow and uncertain. 'It wasn't in the Sirius building. It was an apartment on Queen street.'

It takes a moment for my fatigued brain to process this. Could the barista be wrong? It's a distinct building, capped with a large star shape. It was built recently and is the second tallest building in the city. Hard to forget that. He had it all planned, a penthouse hideout. I reach into my bag and feel for the familiar shape of my car keys.

'Get someone to the Sirius now.'

'What?'

I turn to Gabe, his eyes half-closed, slumped in a chair. 'I'll be back soon,' I say. His mouth opens to speak but I don't pause, I just sprint towards the elevator. 'He was living in an apartment there. His ex-girlfriend visited it and she told me.'

'The Sirius in Southbank?'

'Yes! I might lose you, I'm getting in an elevator. Trust me, get officers there now.'

Sure enough when the elevator doors close, the phone cuts out. It stops one level before the car park. A nurse in squelching white shoes gets in. She's turning a box of cigarettes between her thumb and forefinger. I reach forward, impatiently pressing the button to close the elevator doors.

At the basement car park, I run to the car, calling Simms again, but there is no answer. I call triple zero instead.

'Hi,' I say. 'The kidnapper who is missing, Nathan Schultz, is at the Sirius building in Southbank. Please send police there now.'

The operator asks for more details but I can't give her any. She assures me someone will be on their way.

I pay for parking at the boom gate, then emerge out onto the street. The building is not so far away. Ten minutes if traffic is clear. I'm in the car, flying out towards Southbank. I think of his words. They ring in my mind again.

If I ever lost her, I'd grab a taxi and take the next flight out. I wouldn't hesitate.

I park up outside the building and climb out. My heart is knocking. I scan the street, waiting to see police cars arriving but my hope is already wilting. There are so many people already awake, going about their morning business. He's probably left already.

I see someone. It looks just like him. He is wearing his hood up, a duffel bag slung over his shoulder. He's rushing towards the road, from the entrance of the Sirius. He looks flustered. *It's him.* And the police aren't here yet. He's in a rush. I can hear distant sirens. He has the scanner; he must have been listening. He knows they're coming. Now I see him throw one hand in the air, waving at a passing cab. It doesn't stop. He rushes across the road, weaving between the cars.

Then he is on the other side of the road, striding quickly, his head down and arms pumping. The sirens are coming closer, but they're too late, the street is getting too busy already with cars and pedestrians. Anger boils inside me, making me forget for a moment about the trembling fatigue in my arms and legs. I climb out of the car and rush into the traffic. A horn blares. I make it to the middle.

Trapped there, I watch Cormac disappear down a side street. A momentary break in the cars, I bolt across. More horns but I make it up onto the curb and run the way he had gone. Turning down the side street, I hear a woman's voice on a speaker. *The next train to depart is the 9.05 City Line, stopping all stations to Flinders Street.*

I rush towards the entrance and down the steps to the platform. My hand slides along the handrail. At the bottom of the steps I turn. He's there. I'm frozen for a moment, just watching him, reliving all those conversations. The hours I spent trying to help him. He's looking down at his phone while a dozen or so people on the platform all do the same. I find my eyes fixed on Cormac's back. He's probably organising a flight right now.

He has money, charm, all the means at his disposal to harass me and my family for the rest of his life. Even if the police caught him, he will find a way to get at me. It won't stop. I glance back up towards the street. No police; they're not going to get him. The train is coming. It will be stopping at the platform in just a few seconds. Then he could go anywhere, to the airport, to another city, to another apartment hidden away somewhere. If he gets on that train, he will disappear. I stop thinking about it. I step forward. There is only one thing to do.

Now

THIRTY-FOUR

YESTERDAY I SPENT the afternoon with my lawyer Rebecca, running through the events that led up to that moment. Pushing Cormac, seeing the explosion of blood and bone, the train screaming to a stop. The thud of boots as the police rushed down the ramp, slamming me onto the concrete, cold cuffs against the chafed skin of my wrists.

The video from the CCTV on the platform was shared widely on social media and people like Joe, or doing what Joe used to do, were tasked with filtering it out along with all the other content that breaches their standards. The CCTV footage limits my defence options in the trial.

My nights are mostly sleepless and when I do dream it's about Cormac. I wake with a cool dampness on my spine and his voice in my head. The dreams are always the same: he's there in my old office sitting across from me, asking me those questions. He was always asking questions. Then when he leaves, I follow him through the streets until we're on the train platform. It always ends the same way. Sometimes a conversation first, sometimes he pleads with me, but the train always arrives.

Despite the dreams, the hard prison bed, the dry meat and waterlogged vegetables they serve every day, despite it all, I still don't feel any regret. I had to do it. *I had to.* Cormac tried to kill me. He wouldn't stop until he had killed us all. It was either my family or him.

Rebecca and her assistant have been reviewing the evidence submitted by the prosecution. We've gone through all of the journal entries the police found after the fire, piecing together that night with Peter all those years ago. The prosecution are hoping to show that I am of dubious character, that I not only killed Nathan Schultz in cold blood, but I pushed his father to suicide. They want the judge to believe I am cold and calculating. Rebecca is confident that if we can break this chain of logic, and show it wasn't a considered action but an impulsive one, then we should see the charges downgraded.

With any luck I'll only be in here for a few years. That's a lot of time to reflect. I've read studies about what incarceration does to the human mind, the distance from loved ones, the isolation and boredom.

As well as Gabe, July and Evan, I have had another visitor lately: Joe. Even I was surprised at first when he turned up, but it has been good for me to see him. He was released, cleared of all charges and I imagine he has a good compensation case for being wrongly accused and imprisoned. He seems a changed man. More gracious, philosophical almost. Life is different for him now. He's stopped drinking altogether and his wife has him going with her to mass again. He was so angry before, but now, he says, he forgives me. He's not going back to working in content moderation; that's behind him. He's going to retrain in something else. Oddly, he wants to be a bus driver, or maybe even a train operator.

Joe's visits help. They make me feel like I'm still normal. He drives all the way out here to see me, bringing me a notepad and a pen, so I can continue taking my notes for my lecture. I know I'll never be able to deliver it. No university would want me speaking, even when I get out. But something odd happened when I began to read through all my notes. Something resonated with me. Psychologists always find it difficult to diagnose themselves. Joe printed out and brought me in a copy of the *Antisocial Personality Disorder* test. I opened the first page, held my pen there for a moment. It's a little like those questions my father asked with that look of concern that made the line between his eyes deepen. I find myself thinking about my past a lot more now.

I'm there again outside Peter's bathroom door. I turned back to find the officers were just out of earshot. I knew I only had a few minutes at most before they pulled me away. I knew there was a good chance he would use the gun, but I was in too deep by that stage; there was too much on the line. I hadn't even reported the fact he had the gun.

'Leave me alone, Margot. If you're not here for me, if you don't want me, then clear off. You can't talk me out of it.'

'I know,' I say, quietly, gently. 'I'm here to *support* you, Peter. Support your decision.'

'Support me?'

'I don't think you will do it otherwise. I don't think you will have the courage to pull the trigger.'

'You want this? You want me to do this?'

I thought about how unstable he was, how my career would end if it ever came out we were in a relationship. I thought about my father, the way he could cut right to the core of my inadequacies. I imagined his expression if he found out I'd lost my right to practise. I didn't love Peter, I knew that, but he loved me and an unstable man in love is a dangerous thing.

'It'll never get better. The darkness will never go away. It won't hurt, Peter. Not even a little. Just aim the barrel at the roof of your mouth and pull the trigger.'

A sob. A moment that stretched out like a lifetime. Then the sound of the shot.

I look down at the test then close it again and drop my pen on the stainless-steel table. Sometimes it's best not to know.

Read on for an extract from J.P. Pomare's upcoming title

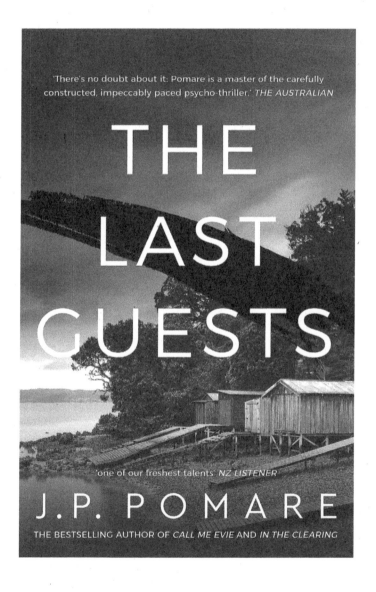

'There's no doubt about it: Pomare is a master of the carefully constructed, impeccably paced psycho-thriller.' THE AUSTRALIAN

THE LAST GUESTS

'one of our freshest talents' NZ LISTENER

J.P. POMARE

THE BESTSELLING AUTHOR OF CALL ME EVIE AND IN THE CLEARING

PROLOGUE

HIS HEART IS steady, his hand is still as he punches the code into the silver lock box bolted to the brick wall near the front door of 299 Hillview Terrace, right where it is supposed to be. Four-one-three-nine, then it falls open and he's staring at a simple silver key attached to a key ring in the shape of New Zealand. He's sweating in the heat, with a coat on, a hat and black leather gloves. There's CCTV on the corner near the milk bar, but he came in the long way, going all the way around the park at the top of the street.

He pockets the key, pulls his hat lower and walks back to the rental parked on the street. He opens the boot, pulls out two large suitcases and wheels them back to the house. He scans the entrance. *No cameras, no surveillance.*

He slides the key into the lock and opens the door then drags the suitcases inside. Open plan, as sterile and neat as a hotel room. Polished floorboards knock beneath the heel of his boots as he passes through the kitchen to the lounge. Framed Ikea prints. A boxy couch that looks like it belongs in a furniture showroom.

Beige rug. Outside, through the ranch slider a tiled courtyard with a potted lemon tree sits in the lukewarm sunlight.

He checks out the other rooms. There's a study just large enough for a pine desk, a chair and a bookshelf. The bedroom is generous: a king-sized bed, as promised, a flat screen TV bolted to the wall and a wardrobe. He knows the place is booked this weekend and most nights next week, which makes sense; it's cheap ($155 a night, including the cleaning fee), central and neat, and there's not enough places in the city to go around. This place averages seven bookings a month. Most importantly, it's available for single-night bookings. Ideal for a one-night stand. Perfect for his needs.

He lays both suitcases down in the living room and opens them to reveal a handheld vacuum cleaner, white cardboard boxes, a cordless drill, screws, screwdrivers, chisels. He also has a plaster kit and a small tin of paint. Using a flathead screwdriver, he opens the paint. He stares into the tin, then at the wall, then into the tin. You can't tell until it dries what colour it will be, but it looks like a perfect match. He'd been worried he might have to go back to the hardware store but that won't be necessary.

His eyes scan the walls and the ceiling once more. His gaze comes to rest on the black pendant light fitting hanging down. Lights are good; people tend not to stare directly at lights. He takes one of the four dining chairs gathered about the table and places it at the centre of the room before climbing up to examine the elaborate bowl-shaped design of the lampshade. He lowers himself back to the carpet again and pulls a portable stereo from one of the suitcases. He puts on music, 'Paint it Black' by The Rolling Stones. With the volume up high he takes the drill. The two-millimetre bit is already fitted. He climbs onto the chair again, holds the light in place with one hand, wields the tool with the other hand and begins drilling a tiny aperture. It's an expensive tool, quiet, much quieter than the splash of the cymbals, the rolling thud of the base drum. He hums the tune.

Back down from the chair, he opens the boxes, looking for the size he is after. *Bingo.* Three millimetre, fish eye lens. He removes the camera, about the size of a pen nib. He climbs back up, presses it through the hole in the light fitting and fastens it in place. He blows on the lens, thumbs the sleeve of his shirt over it then returns to the floor and inspects his handiwork. Unless you knew what you were looking for, you would never notice it.

Next he goes to the bedroom, eyes searching once more. The lamp could work but lying in bed it would be at eye level. He tilts his head to look at the ceiling. There's a smoke alarm. He could punch out the LED light and put the camera eye in its place. He brings the chair in from the lounge room, climbs up, unclips the smoke alarm then sets about inserting the camera into it. The alarm won't work anymore – he takes the battery out just to be sure – but once he's reattached it to the ceiling it looks exactly like it did before.

He stops at the door of the bathroom, considers the layout for a moment. He surveys the walls, his gloved hands gently sliding across the tiles. He knows he has to put a camera in here, but there is no obvious location. If he puts one in the ceiling beside the fan, the steam would likely obscure the vision. There is no one spot that will capture both the shower and the rest of the room. The only option, in that case, is two separate cameras – preferably in places the steam won't reach. He runs hot water in the shower with the fan running, watches where the steam comes to rest on the surfaces. The glass of the shower screen, the mirror, the steel handrail beside the toilet. Anywhere lower than waist height is safe from fogging the lens. The towel rail is attached to the wall with a small screw. That'll do. He has a camera mounted in a screw head; it wasn't cheap or easy to find but he's glad he spent the extra money now.

He carefully removes the screw from the towel rail and replaces it with the camera. Then he places the second camera in the light fitting above the mirror, just below the fan.

When he has installed all the cameras, he finds the crawl space access. He drops one cable down through the light fitting in the lounge, another into the smoke alarm in the bedroom, runs a third along the wall to the towel rail and the light fitting in the bathroom. The switch board just inside the front door opens to reveal a panel of new circuit breakers. He runs all the cables from the cameras down through the same switch as the hot water service.

The walls are thin plasterboard. Tapping with his knuckles he finds the stud near the meter box and cuts a small hole beside it with a jab saw; the hole is just large enough for his remote-access wireless router which is already configured with the cameras. He can't stream through the complimentary wi-fi lest the hosts change the password or have enough technical nous to check how many devices are currently connected to the network and realise there are four extras unaccounted for – the four cameras. Some savvy travellers have apps and devices which check to see if any cameras are running through local wi-fi networks.

He installs a power point within the wall and plugs the router in. Then he takes a piece of plaster from his kit and cuts it to shape, fitting it into the hole to hide the router. He's a perfectionist. It's a fault as much as an advantage; he can't leave a job until everything is polished, finished. He considers everything that could go wrong and devises ways to mitigate the risk, going above and beyond. Fail to prepare, prepare to fail. Those things he can't account for are what keeps him up at night. It's in his genes. He was restless as a kid but came into his own in his teenage years. As an adult, what calms him most is sanding down a jag in a wooden bench or buffing out a scuff in floorboards. He's had a few jobs, that's the way of the world now, but this job has made him the most money; this work is, oddly, the most satisfying. There is enough risk to keep it interesting, but when you're as careful and precise there's almost no chance of getting caught.

Now he mixes a little plaster and smears it over the seams of the replaced plasterboard. While it dries he goes back to the kitchen bench. Opening his tablet, he logs into the surveillance software.

The screen shows a man in a cap hunched over a faux stone benchtop in a terrace house in Auckland city, with boxes open on the carpet of the lounge nearby. He clicks through the streams: the bathroom, a view of the shower and then a view of the toilet, then the bedroom.

'Shit,' he says to himself. 'You idiot.'

The bedroom camera catches only two-thirds of the bed. He can see everything except the pillows. Looking down at the tablet on the kitchen bench, he grinds the heels of his palms into his temples. The bed yields the most sought-after footage – that's why he is here. He strides back into the room, searching for a better spot. He could shift the smoke detector, sand and paint where it was, rewire it to the new spot. But a cleaner might notice if the smoke alarm has moved; a nosey cleaner might even take a closer look. That's the easiest way to lose his equipment and possibly get caught. *I could turn the fitting so the camera is aimed closer to the bed*, he decides.

He brings the chair back in and climbs up to start turning the alarm fitting. As he examines it, though, he realises the smoke alarm wasn't removed last time the room was painted and it has a smear of paint on one side. It's dusty, too, clearly a few years old and now that he has handled it he sees where his gloved fingers have made small marks. He chews his lips, his frustration growing. Should he put a second camera in this room? But where? *How many viewers will I lose if I don't have the pillows in the frame?* He thinks. No one is bringing full HD streams with night vision, so it doesn't matter if you miss the pillows; the viewers will still flood his streams. He wipes the dust away on the chest of his shirt, and climbs down.

It'll have to do. By the time he has vacuumed and cleaned, his repairs are dry. In the kitchen near the front door, he lays out a sheet of newspaper, takes the paint and the paintbrush out. He studies the wall for a moment, noting the original paintwork, the telling strokes. It was clearly a roller, decent paint that has been there for a while. His tin is enough for ten square metres. Easily enough to do the entire wall if he needed to. He thinks for a moment, considering it. He has drop sheets with him. The fine sandpaper makes a pleasing rasping sound as he smooths the edges of the new plaster. Then he cleans it with an alcohol wipe, fills the paint roller and begins rolling it on. He won't be able to tell if it is perfect until it dries. For now, he packs up most of the boxes into his suitcases. When he cranes his head out the front door, he finds the street empty. He quickly drags the suitcases back out to the rental car, stowing them away in the boot.

He starts the car and drives up the street, once again avoiding the CCTV near the corner shop. He heads north, over the harbour bridge and west to a part of the city where no one would ever recognise him. Where people don't ask questions of strangers or remember faces. He takes off his gloves now.

The man at the hardware store is grinding a key when he walks in, so he waits with his head down, pretending to study a display of key rings near the counter. The grinder stops, the man blows away the steel files and looks down at the keys he has cut, walking towards the counter. 'How can I help you?'

'I just need this cut.' He holds out the key. 'This is the wife's copy.'

'Lost yours, eh?' He takes the key, peers closely at it.

He answers quickly, the first thing that comes to mind. 'Mine is at the bottom of the Pacific.'

'Right,' the man says with a smile. 'Fisherman.'

'You bet.'

'Give me ten minutes. Just one?'

'Sorry?'

'One copy, yeah?'

'One's fine.'

'It'll be five bucks.'

He smiles. 'That's fine.'

He goes back to the car park, sits in the car to wait for the key, watching the camera streams on his phone. With the curtains closed and the bedroom dark, he turns on night mode. The screen goes from black to a shade of green like something at the bottom of the sea. The shape of the bed is clear, the pattern on the carpet – it's good. Much clearer than he was expecting.

The key is ready and waiting for him when he returns to the hardware store.

He picks it up, finds a tiny buoy attached to the key ring.

'Now it'll float,' the man says with a wink.

'Thanks,' he says, annoyed that he is making himself more memorable. Easy to imagine this chipper bloke in a dim police interview room. *Yeah, the fisherman. I remember him clearly.* He should be more careful than this. In the future he *will* be more careful.

He pays cash, pockets the key, and returns to the car.

Back at the house, wearing his gloves and hat once more, he tests the key and finds it slides in and turns smoothly. The door unlocks. He can return whenever he wants. Some months from now, when the place isn't booked, he can slip inside and uninstall the cameras.

The paint has dried and the patch is indistinct from the rest of the wall. He packs up the last of his things, pulls a chair out, half closes the curtains, tips a third of the complimentary bottle of milk down the sink. He pulls a small ziplock bag from his pocket and opens it to pluck out one of the long blonde hairs inside. He lays it on a pillow. He'd collected them from the drain at a swimming pool across town.

He pulls the blankets back on the bed and rumples the sheets. He empties the remaining five hairs in the ziplock bag into the shower, then he runs the hot water for a moment. He mops up a little of the water with one of the towels then leaves it on the floor. He does one last walk through, eyes searching for any sign that he has been here, but everything is in place.

In the glow from the streetlight he locks the keys away, as per the instructions on the Airbnb listing, and gets into the rental car. He can come back again, so long as the place isn't booked, so long as no one is here. Tomorrow morning the hosts will receive a message letting them know he has checked out. Then it will be a matter of waiting.

PART ONE

1

'LINA' CAIN SAYS.

A current shoots down my spine. I'm deleting the app before he has a chance to see what it is. When that tiny blue app disappears from my screen, I turn my head back.

'Yeah?'

'What are you doing?'

I turn the rest of my body now, phone still squeezed in my fist. 'Oh, nothing. I just downloaded the wrong app.'

'Right,' he says, he's in his towel and the shower is already running. He takes up his protein shaker and gives it a few pumps. 'I'll be quick in the shower, are you ready?'

'Yeah,' I say, my voice a little tight. 'Almost.' I notice a slight tremble in my hand holding the phone, and I look at it as if my eyes will keep it still. Thankfully he doesn't seem to notice as he drains the liquid, the muscles in his throat working. He has clipped his hair again, a few millimetres of salted black. The towel is loose on his waist and it's clear now beneath the kitchen downlights he has trimmed up. He's getting his SAS body back, but it's more than that, more mass, a bulging chest and shoulders.

'Love you,' he says, stepping closer now, laying a kiss on my forehead.

Everyone has secrets, I tell myself as my palm and fingers begin to ache around my phone. And it's true. Or is it just one of those things people, bad people, tell themselves? Whispering little lies to get through the days. It's easy to do wrong, the trick is learning to live with it. And secrets, *most* secrets, are harmless. A secret like mine is a snake in a box, so long as it stays inside it can't hurt, right?

Cain is back out of the shower now. I watch him get dressed, his body mapped with pale scars up his left side, concentrating between his knee and hip, with those slashes reaching up to his shoulder. Surgeons cut out most of the shrapnel and his body has since squeezed more of it out, but there are still scraps encased in knots of scar tissue that'll be in there until he dies.

Now he picks up the iron and slides it over his shirt then pulls it on. I adjust his collar, find it still warm. A smile now. And those dimples bracketing his mouth, almost too charming for his weathered, rugged face. Three and a half decades of life are carved in faint lines about his eyes. He's still handsome, shopworn and creased but a strong jaw, eyes that catch the light. I feel both love and guilt, heat in my chest and ice in my gut.

'You set for work later?' he asks.

'Yep, I've got my uniform in the car.'

Axel and Claire's house is about twenty-five minutes south-east of the CBD, a big two-storey place with neighbours who all work in the city and labradors in most the yards. Then there is Axel and Claire, who fit in like black nail polish on a beauty queen. Cain reaches for my car keys and I volunteer them. It's a small kindness from him to drive when he can. I spend half my day driving – people think an ambulance officer's job is performing CPR and administering epi-pens when really we spend much more time navigating through traffic and waiting in car parks for call outs.

Cain steers us through the streets to the motorway south, soon we are pulling off again, and rolling through the tree-lined streets.

'Knock, knock,' I call through the screen door when we have arrived. 'Hello.'

'Come in,' Axel's deep voice calls. 'It's unlocked.' We walk through to the living room, white walls, pale timber floorboards. The sort of place that looks barely lived in at all. I suppose they have a cleaner, it was probably one of those decisions that are easy for people with money. *Should we get a cleaner? Do you know anyone good? Why don't we find out who the Smiths use?*

'Hello lovelies,' Claire says, striding to Cain first for a hug. 'Jesus you need to chill out on the bench press.'

'Tell me about it,' I say.

Taj, the twelve-year-old beagle, comes over at her heels.

Claire hugs me, kisses the air beside my cheek. She calls herself the yogoth – bottle-black hair, beetle shell nails and tattoos – she also has her own Yoga studio in the city. I've gone along once or twice, always a mixed bag when it comes to customers.

'I love your hair,' she says.

'I've gone short.'

'Very short, very chic.' She might as well be complimenting her own hair, which is shorter than mine, darker and undeniably *more* chic. But I appreciate it. Claire is one of the good ones, partial to a buttery chardonnay and is always kind and free for a chat. We'd caught up for wine a few times when the boys were away. We'd joked about getting matching tattoos. *WW.* War wives. It was nice to have a confidante, someone I could talk to about what Cain did, other than the dismissive '*he's in the army.*' The canned response to most people who had asked, avoiding those follow-up questions. It's an SAS thing. You'd think he was James Bond.

Axel comes over in his apron with Michelangelo's David on the front. He's not as tall as Cain but otherwise they could be twins. He and Cain's hands clap together, palms thump backs.

Axel steps back now, gives me that grin that belongs on a salesman, or a politician. Dentist-white teeth, year-round tan. He's not vain but he looks after himself, in designer jeans tight around his muscled thighs and a loose linen shirt. Hard to imagine him as an elite soldier nowadays.

'You're a fine wine, Lina. Better every year.'

'Eventually wine turns rancid,' I joke.

'That's true. You're not there yet though. Speaking of which. Wine, beer?' he says it like a question pointing at each of us.

'Not for me,' I say. 'I got called in. Shift starts at eleven.'

'You're joking?' Claire says now. 'It's been so long since we got drunk together.'

'No,' I say. 'I wish I was joking but I've got to do it.'

'Lina, why are you picking up extra shifts? You work too hard. Unlike this one,' Axel teases Cain, gently jabbing his shoulder.

We're broke, hardly the answer they want. Not *technically* true but COVID-19 hit us as hard as anyone. 'Oh, I'm just trying to help out where I can.'

'Can't someone else do it?'

'No, I owed a favour and already said yes. Too late to pull out now.'

'Well, in that case do you want a glass of juice, or we've got ginger beer?' Claire offers.

'Oh no, I'm fine really,' I say. I've tried so often to cut back on my drinking. Alcoholism is in my genes, it seems at times inevitable. It wasn't until we began trying for a kid that I really got on top of it. And now I barely touch alcohol at all. The only people I seem to drink around are these two, Claire and Axel. Black belts in peer pressure, both of them.

'So, we have a proposition,' Claire begins. 'How would you two feel about looking after Taj next weekend?'

Cain flicks a glance towards me then back to Claire. 'Why?'

'We're Airbnbing our place out, otherwise he's going to the kennels.'

A spark in Cain's eyes. 'Oh, that's right you mentioned it,' he says to Axel. 'That's this weekend, is it?'

'Yep. Check in Friday afternoon. I *personally* think the kennels are okay, but Claire calls them the gulags,' Axel teases, spearing a carrot on his plate.

'I call them the gulags *in private,* thank you very much. But he does come home with the shakes.'

'They must be giving him electric shock therapy and charging us $70 a night. You'd be doing us a huge favour. We could just give you two the money.'

Seventy *a night?* To look after a dog? I don't really want it in our house. Cain asks me with his eyes, shrugging, before he can respond I speak. 'No,' I say. 'We're actually going to Tarawera for the weekend.' The lie comes easily.

Cain is still staring at me, he quirks an eyebrow.

'Sorry, Taj,' Claire says, her exaggerated vowels stolen from a bad TV drama. 'They don't love you.'

'Why can't you take him away?'

'Mum's allergies,' Claire says, resting an elbow on the table and cupping her chin in her palm. 'And he hates the car. Are you sure you don't want to go to Tarawera *next* weekend instead?' She tips a little wine into her mouth, her jaw-length black hair falling to one side. She's exquisite. Small and strong. When we'd holidayed together in Bali a few years ago, Axel and Claire drew stares everywhere we went. Skin as tight as stretched rubber, muscles stencilled just below the surface. After a boozy day poolside, I had let my eyes linger on Axel in the water for just a heartbeat too long, more fascinated than anything else but Cain had noticed. 'I'm sure he wouldn't mind if you took a picture.'

'No,' I say. 'They're just both so bloody fit.'

He'd raised his eyebrows as if to say tell me about it.

'Like you,' I'd added a beat too late. 'You are all ripped and here I sit, a doughy profiterole.'

The memory reminds me of the app, Cain in the kitchen. *What are you doing?* Had he seen it? I realise they're all waiting for me to speak again. 'No,' I say. 'We can't go next weekend, I've got work. Wish we could help but we've not been down to check in on the lake house in a while and I really wanted to get there this weekend.'

'Off to the gulag again, sorry Taj,' Claire says.

'So anyone can book this place at any time?' Cain asks, changing the subject.

'No, people can only book the weekends we make it available,' Axel says. 'The Marathon is on here so we're getting three hundred a night.' That perfect smile is on full beam now, and I wonder for just a second if he had braces to get his teeth so straight. 'I've been telling you Caino, it's money for old rope.'

'Three hundred dollars?' I ask, blinking. It's a lot; this place is modern and well styled, I guess. More comfortable than a hotel room.

'It's booked out for three nights.'

'You could put Taj up in a penthouse in Sky City for that.'

Claire begins packing up the plates. 'You guys should rent your lake house out,' she says.

'I've been telling Cain that for years,' Axel says.

Cain gives me a look. I know why he's never raised it, he knows that it is more than a house to me.

'Have you done it before, rented this place out?' I ask.

'Loads,' Claire says, stepping back towards the table. 'Probably half a dozen times over the past couple of years. We just go away when they're here. We set our price quite high.'

'I don't know if I could do it at home,' I say. 'Have people going through my things. *Anyone* could be staying. What if they did something?'

Axel swallows a mouthful of wine, he drags his smile up on one side. '*Lina, Lina, Lina.* This is the twenty-first century, you can't cash a cheque or rent a pushbike without a retina scan, laying down your life savings as a deposit, a blood bond to hand over your first born and nine different forms of ID.'

Cain laughs. They all do. I try to be polite, push a smile to my lips. 'I know but—'

'It's not so simple as just whipping up a profile and making the booking.' He gestures with his wine glass as he speaks. 'They hold a deposit, confirm ID and offer a lot of support to hosts. We've never had a problem. Hell, I'd even set it all up for you if you wanted.'

'What about you?' I say, turning to Cain, hoping for backup. 'Would you do it?'

Cain chews his lips for a moment. 'I don't trust strangers. But it's good money, and we could do with a little more.' That's the understatement of the year.

'If you're worried about people going through your stuff, lock it away. You could make a fortune. A place on the lake, market it as an artist's retreat, or a quiet family weekend away and just get some income?'

'What if someone, I don't know, decided to cook meth in your house?'

Axel takes a sip of his wine, pauses with the glass close to his lips. 'That only happens on TV,' he says to me.

I continue. 'Or what if they go through your things and steal your passports? What if they cut your keys?'

'And come back to murder us?' His bark of laughter grates, it's dismissive as if the idea of him, elite soldier, being vulnerable were outside the realms of possibility.

I want to remind them all about the news story from a few months ago. The murder, somewhere in the states. That was an Airbnb wasn't it? Either way I want to mention it but by the time I've ordered my thoughts, the conversation is moving again and it would seem petty to try bring it up now.

'Tell them about the knickers?' Claire speaks with laugher in her voice.

'Knickers?' Cain says.

Axel laughs, covers his eyes with his palm. 'It's nothing.'

'What's this?' I say. 'I love a knickers story.'

'Don't scare them off, Claire, we can get a referral fee if they do it.' *Referral fee, is that the agenda here?*

'It's not much of a story. Just something we found,' Claire says, dismissing her husband with the flick of her wrist.

'Knickers,' Axel says. 'Tiny, lacy knickers.'

'No,' I say, slowly, my hand coming to my mouth.

'Yep. Scrunched up down the side of the bed when we were cleaning after someone left.'

'What sort?' Cain asks.

'Gross,' I say. 'It doesn't matter what sort.'

'A lacy G-string,' Claire deadpans, her green eyes fixing Cain.

'We were tempted to contact the guests to return them for a laugh,' Axel adds.

'People have sex in your bed and leave their knickers behind?' Cain says. 'And pay you for the privilege.'

'Airbnb is an alternative to hotels and what's one of the main reason people hire hotel rooms? To have sex with someone they shouldn't,' Claire says.

Cain glances across the table at that moment to me, again a question on his face. 'Do you change your pillowcases and everything?' he asks.

'Oh yeah, we change our pillows even.'

'Sounds foolproof.'

I try now, once more to bring up the incident in the US. 'What about those rumours, people stealing art and replacing it with replicas, or . . . you know. The other thing?' I say.

'What thing?' Axel says, hunching over the table, resting on his forearms.

'A man was killed in an Airbnb. He recorded it and shared the footage, remember?'

'Oh that? Yeah that wasn't Airbnb's fault. Some psychopath just wanted to kill someone.'

Cain is looking down at his phone. 'Lina,' he says, pausing the conversation. 'There's a three-bedroom place on the lake for three hundred a night. We've got more bedrooms. *And*,' he says scrolling with his thumb, 'better views by the looks of it.'

I hold out my hand. 'Let me see.' It's the big house, with the steep driveway up on the hill. Walking distance from the Anglers but not on the water like ours. 'The house is nicer but we're in a better spot.' I see all the other listings dotted around the lakes area. Lots of people are doing it apparently.

'Oh,' Claire interrupts. 'Lina you've not seen the terrace.'

'It's finished?'

'Come on,' she says. 'Let's have a look.' She leads me outside onto their deck, up a set of steps. As I follow her the city emerges from beyond the other rooftops, an entire landscape before us. All those lights, bushfire embers in the darkness. We reach the terrace on the roof of their townhouse. It's fake grass and deck chairs and I find myself wondering if this addition is in the tens or hundreds of thousands.

'God look at that,' I say.

'It's nice right?' she says. 'Good night for it too.'

'Stunning,' I say, barely keeping the note of envy out of my voice. Claire has a yoga studio and Axel has one of those gyms that's full of ropes, boxes and tractor tyres. He wants to open more, a chain of them, an empire. Axel was the one that put the idea in Cain's head to start his own personal training business; thus *Commando Fitness* was born. The first time Cain told me the name Axel had suggested it was with a cringe. 'I like it,' I'd lied. He still cringes now, whenever he updates his website or Facebook, when someone points out the logo on the skin-tight t-shirts he trains in, the cartoonish muscle man in military fatigues squatting beneath an impossibly bent bell bar. *Commando* emblazoned in block letters above it and *Fitness* below.

He trains people out of Axel's gym, paying a small fee each month to do so. Despite his injuries, the scars and a knee that barely bends, he still manages to keep strong. Suits and yuppies like the idea of training the way the SAS do, that's the gimmick, but Cain's had a hard time gaining new clients and keeping them.

'The guests must love this?'

'This is the first booking we've taken since the renovation,' Claire says. She's got her glass of Chardonnay with her and it's clear from the way she seems to oscillate the glass, almost spilling it, that she's at least halfway drunk. Cool girls, girls like Claire, I had always assumed would drink negronis or craft beer, not the variety of wine I've come to associate with middle-aged housewives.

'Have you guys had any bad reviews?'

A long silence, she takes a sip now and the air becomes thick and cool.

'Not yet,' she says. Then she turns away from the skyline, facing me. 'How are *you* guys going, Lina?'

'Us? We're good,' I say, guarded. There was something off in her tone. She continues watching me, I feel the urge to speak again. 'Cain's good. He seems to enjoy working and it's getting him out of the house, earning again. Takes his mind off things.'

'Good,' she says. 'That's nice.' Her eyes don't leave mine as she takes another gulp of wine. 'Um, can I talk to you about something that might seem a little—' her free hand dances in the air between us '—what's the word . . . gauche?' she says. 'Is that it?'

'I don't know,' I say. 'Depends.'

A moment passes, I see her uncertainty.

'What is it?'

'Look this is a little awkward for me, Lina, but I know you guys are struggling at the moment.'

'What do you mean?' Is this about money or something else?

'I mean . . . well, I know Axel won't bring it up directly with Cain. His approach is to throw money at problems but it's not so simple.'

'Umm sorry what is it—'

'Look you don't have to tell me what's going on. It's just Axel's gym is at capacity, and he's giving up some of his own clients for Cain,' she says, and I can see the colour in her cheeks. She's holding her glass in two hands but takes one off to twist a finger at the corner of her eye. 'Axel told me Cain has had a couple of arguments with people at the gym, he snapped at one of the regulars about taking too long using a chin up bar that Cain was waiting for. I guess I'm wondering if everything is okay with him?'

He has been moody lately, I've noticed. Not as bad as that year after he returned, when he was going to physio three times a week, taking handfuls of painkillers and antidepressants.

'He's doing okay,' I say. 'Maybe he's just been a little bit off the last few weeks.'

'Yeah,' she says. 'Well, Axel wants to open a second gym and after this renovation money has become really tight for us. I'm sure when he stopped charging Cain to use his space it helped but now he wants to give Cain a loan, to help him get things moving.'

I can feel blood rushing to my own cheeks. Axel isn't charging Cain any more? So what overheads does Cain have? 'But Cain's business is doing okay,' I say. 'What do you mean get things moving?'

She doesn't say the word *oh* but her mouth forms the shape, those perfect eyebrows rise up her forehead.

'Claire,' I say, my voice firm now.

'Shit.' She clamps a hand to her forehead, swings her head away then back to me. 'I thought maybe you knew.' She tosses her free hand as if dismissing the entire conversation. 'It wasn't my place to say anything. Let the boys figure it out, I don't know why I brought it up. Pretend I never said anything. Please?'

And how on earth would I do that, Claire? 'Oh,' I say. 'I mean yeah, I knew the business was struggling but he doesn't need a loan.' I feel sick thinking about it. *No secrets,* he promised. But is this a secret?

Claire looks sad for a moment. She knows I'm lying.

'Yeah,' she says. 'I know you did. Oh, I've put my foot in it, haven't I? I just wanted to make sure he was okay. You know what those boys are like, they never say what they mean.'

I turn and try to smile. 'Sure. Let's head back in shall we?' I check my phone. It's almost time to go.

The boys look up from an iPad as we enter the house. Their conversation stops now, do they know something is going on? 'What's up?' Cain says, the booze melting the 't' in 'what's'.

'Nothing, I was just admiring the view out there. Incredible, Axel. You guys have done such a good job with the renovation.'

'We're still talking about Airbnb,' Axel says. 'I've almost convinced him.'

So Cain can start making his own money? I think to myself. I feel a pang of frustration slap the back of my neck. *That's probably what this is about, they're trying to help us make money, they know we are broke.* I think back to something Cain had told me about Axel. 'He's like my older brother, he'd never let me get into trouble.' What if Axel sees things differently? What if Cain isn't like a brother, but a liability?

'It's not him that needs convincing I'm sorry to say.'

I can see that serious mind behind Cain's eyes turning over the idea. A decision is already made as far as he is concerned and my objections are the only thing between him and a new way to make money. We never should have ended up here, like this in the city. Treading water financially, in a place we don't love, doing work we resent. The plan was, *no* the plan *is* to move to Tarawera, without the big city rent and expenses, to begin raising a family, quiet and still as the lake. We'd be there now, if it wasn't for me. If I'd not failed. If I'd not lost the baby.

Peephole transmission

Live streams will resume from this coming Sunday with new precautions in place to prevent occupants of the Peepholes from being doxed or harassed. Planters no longer need to hold footage for twenty-four hours before publishing to the platform, but given the recent events in Colorado we will continue to monitor the situation closely. We still maintain our main focus is to protect the identities of our planters and subscribers. As always, members of our community in breach of any of the rules will be punished. Streams will return permanently provided there is no further scrutiny of our service from authorities and investigative bodies.

Please enjoy the show.

ACKNOWLEDGEMENTS

THIS BOOK WOULDN'T exist without the generous insights into the world of psychology from Marion Barton and Caitlin Kilgour. I'm also deeply grateful to Cohen Morris for helping with procedural matters concerning firefighting and law enforcement.

As always thanks to my agent, Pippa Masson, and everyone at Hachette including the dream team Robert Watkins, Brigid Mullane and Tessa Connelly.

Thanks to Paige for your patience with me and my work.

Finally, a big thanks to my mother-in-law, Jackie. There are few editors as direct and brutally honest as you, and fewer still who will drop everything just to begin reading my messy first drafts the moment I send them.

hachette
AUSTRALIA

If you would like to find out more about Hachette Australia,
our authors, upcoming events and new releases you can visit
our website or our social media channels:

hachette.com.au

 HachetteAustralia

 HachetteAus